"Why are you here?" Hannah asked. **"Have you changed your mind about Tuesday?"**

"No. I just wanted to see you," Colt said.

Her skin grew warm, and she experienced a loose, lifting sensation in her midsection as his gaze roamed over her face, then lingered on her mouth.

To cover her sudden disquiet, she began putting her photographs away. Then she looked directly at him. "Tell me what you want, Colt."

Gazing at her as if he were a starving man at a feast prepared for a king, he murmured, "I want you."

It's too fast, she thought, but her heart seemed to know what was right. She stood like a tree, rooted to the floor, helpless and completely at his mercy. She had no thoughts. She felt incapable of speech or movement. Yet deep within her a life energy surged through her veins, changing who and what she was, altering the world she lived in. And he became the sun and the moon to her.

He put his hand to her cheek, and she leaned into his warmth and intensity, stretching and aching for more. . . .

WHAT ARE *LOVESWEPT* ROMANCES?

They are stories of true romance and touching emotion. We believe those two very important ingredients are constants in our highly sensual and very believable stories in the *LOVESWEPT* line. Our goal is to give you, the reader, stories of consistently high quality that may sometimes make you laugh, sometimes make you cry, but are always fresh and creative and contain many delightful surprises within their pages.

Most romance fans read an enormous number of books. Those they truly love, they keep. Others may be traded with friends and soon forgotten. We hope that each *LOVESWEPT* romance will be a treasure—a "keeper." We will always try to publish

LOVE STORIES YOU'LL NEVER FORGET
BY AUTHORS YOU'LL ALWAYS REMEMBER

The Editors

Loveswept® 506

Mary Kay McComas
To Give a Heart Wings

BANTAM BOOKS
NEW YORK · TORONTO · LONDON · SYDNEY · AUCKLAND

TO GIVE A HEART WINGS

A Bantam Book / November 1991

If you would be interested in receiving protective vinyl
covers for your Loveswept books, please write to this address
for information:

Loveswept
Bantam Books
P.O. Box 985
Hicksville, NY 11802

ISBN 0-553-44197-3

Published simultaneously in the United States and Canada

My thanks to fellow writer Martha Butler,
whose faith in me and enthusiasm for this story
made *not* writing it an impossibility.

A special thank you to Dennis Bucher,
who very kindly kept me on track—so to speak.

And last but not least—to Cheryl Heppner,
who graciously allowed me to fumble about
in her world, teaching and advising me with
incredible patience and understanding,
I dedicate this book.

One

Late April was off-season at the beach, but no one seemed to notice. The hour was late, but no one seemed to care. Flynn's Bar was teeming with merrymakers, and it was time to party.

The music blared, vibrating the walls. The locals rocked elbow to elbow on the large dance floor with the spectacular backdrop of the Atlantic ocean beyond.

From the balcony that circled the main floor, a cocktail napkin twirled and spiraled downward over the heads of the sprightly crowd below. It fluttered and drifted slightly to the right, floating briefly on an air current before it skimmed across Hannah Alexander's table and landed on the floor beside her.

Hannah had watched the napkin's descent and automatically looked up to see if a cocktail would follow. One glass stood out from the rest. It dangled between the long, slim fingers of a man who was leaning casually over the guardrail . . . watching Hannah.

His gaze met and held hers. It was as if he'd been waiting for her to notice him. Now that she had, she was hard put to notice anything else.

His face was familiar, though she knew she'd never met the man. As faces went, his wasn't the most handsome she'd ever seen. His coloring was dark—black hair with sun-weathered skin. Strong angular features were saved from being harsh by a touch of humor, a sort of supersensitive understanding of nature, that lurked about the edges of his eyes. He had a moustache, too, she noticed. It lent him the air of a scamp.

She liked his body posture. She made a living exploring shapes, forms, and angles, and his were very interesting. He looked strong and healthy from what she could see. But there was something in the way he held himself, in the tilt of his head and the loose curve of his shoulders, that declared his power to be in his brain, not in his brawn.

Out of necessity, Hannah had spent a great deal of her life developing a keen intuition about people. She had an eye for seeing through the front that protected or disguised the real person underneath. This man was easier to read than most. He didn't appear to be hiding anything about himself. His attitude said, "If you like me, I'll try to like you back. If you don't, it's no skin off my nose."

Judging by the festivities on the upper tier, he didn't seem to have a problem making friends. He was surrounded by people and obviously controlled a large part of the focus of attention. Still, he casually waved off one person after another during the long moments that his gaze remained firmly fixed on Hannah.

"You're not celebrating," Trevor McKinnon muttered near his brother's ear as they bent over the banister, shoulder to shoulder, on the upper level of Flynn's.

"Sure I am," Colt said. They'd just signed a new sponsor for next year's Winston Cup Races, which was truly something to celebrate, but his gaze didn't waver from the woman below. "I'm celebrating in silence. I'm as drunk as a skunk, and I've hardly touched this," he said, indicating the drink in his hand.

"Ah-ha. The radar's up, and we're fixed on target zero, I see." He flung a lazy arm across his older brother's shoulder and followed the track of Colt's gaze with his own. "Which one is it? The brunette?"

Colt nodded once. He'd been watching her for quite a while. She was quick and sharp. She hadn't missed anything that had happened at the crowded nightclub, including his trick with the napkin, since she'd arrived. She seemed very aware of everything going on around her, but she wasn't joining in; she wasn't a part of it. Why not? Why wasn't she dancing? Why wasn't she beating men off with a stick? Lord, what a beauty she was.

"Hmm. Nice," Trevor commented from a connoisseur's point of view. "But her friend looks like a drag. Sorry. You're on your own with this one, pal."

Colt nodded again, more to shut Trevor up than for any other reason. In blood and spirit, they were brothers. Professionally, they were partners. There were a hundred things they depended on each other for, but attracting women wasn't one of them, and they both knew it.

He wanted to be alone. He wanted the band to stop playing. He wanted everyone to leave . . . except the woman below. And all he wanted from her was to be allowed to simply look at her. He'd never seen anything like her.

Hannah held his stare. She didn't have any other choice. He commanded it. That alone was an odd sensation. Usually, she wasn't very good at taking orders. But somehow this one was different. It was more like a soft, persistent calling with a gentle "please" on the end. Too compelling to refuse.

At long last he smiled at her, and Flynn's seemed to come to life with a new brightness and cheer. He had a huge, engaging grin with deep, glee-filled dimples in both cheeks. His eyes lit up with an excitement that almost took her breath away. The quick switch from sober-thoughtful to happy-playful stunned her and made the room begin to spin.

He pointed downward in her direction as if he were trying to tell her something.

Hannah looked around her. No one else had noticed the man on the balcony. But just to make sure that he was indeed trying to communicate with her, she placed her hand over her heart and looked back at him in question.

He nodded once, and again motioned downward in her direction. She frowned, unable to grasp his message. When he lightly patted the bottom of his glass, she recalled the cocktail napkin which had first caught her attention. It was the only thing she could think of that was farther down on the floor than she was.

Her gaze followed the path the napkin had taken, and she found it resting beside the leg of her chair. She picked it up and looked back at the man. He was smiling in the most charming manner, as if what she'd done had pleased him.

Hannah continued to frown. Surely he didn't expect her to return his napkin to him? She turned the napkin over in her fingers to see if there was anything about it that made it special.

On the back, in dark, bold print, it read: "You are very beautiful."

She looked up in amazement, and the man smiled back benevolently. Again she had the feeling that she knew the man, but at the same time was positive she didn't.

With the uneasy feeling that she'd intercepted a message meant for someone else, she looked at the women seated at the tables near her. None of them were looking at the man on the balcony.

Feeling more than a little self-conscious, she looked back at the man. There was an appreciation for her discomfort in his eyes, but no sympathy in his smile. He nodded his head at her in a sincere and reaffirming way and mouthed the word "beautiful."

It wasn't until after a warm flush of feeling washed up into her cheeks that Hannah's own sense of humor kicked in. What a ninny, she chastised herself. He was most likely the biggest flirt in the northern hemisphere. She suspected that he dropped flattering notes into crowds everywhere and wooed any woman dumb enough to pick them up.

Well, Hannah had been walked around the block a couple of times before, and clever though his was, she didn't fall for every line that was dangled in front of her. She let her expression tell him that she recognized the sport he was playing and that she wasn't about to get hooked by it. With a polite nod of her head, she thanked him for the incidental compliment, then dismissed him, turning her attention back to her companion for the evening.

Not that Willie was much of a companion at the moment. She was lost in a world of her own. Worse yet, Willie was in love. Not that there was anything wrong with being in love, in general. It was Willie in love that she found slightly tedious.

One of the things Hannah had always liked best about Willie was that it was innately impossible for her to do anything the same way other people did it. If directions indicated one course, she took another and stuck with it single-mindedly until it came out the way she wanted. It was a trait that she had no doubt inherited from her mother, though Willie would rather step on her own tongue than admit it.

However, it was this same idiosyncrasy that Hannah found annoying when Willie chanced to fall in love—which was about twice a month.

She presently sat in a semicomatose state of pure, unadulterated rapture, mesmerized by every nuance of movement, every gesture and expression, every particle of air disturbed by the drummer in the band.

If only he knew, Hannah thought, glancing from Willie's sweet, freckled face to the drummer, who, in a world of *his* own, had no notion of the love and adoration being bestowed on him from afar. On the other hand, maybe he did, she speculated as she watched him wink at someone on the dance floor.

In any event, he wasn't and hadn't been aware of Willie in the two days she'd been mooning over him, and in all honesty, Hannah was growing a little impatient with the situation. She'd come to the beach before the summer crowds gathered for a well-deserved weekend of rest and relaxation, not to nurse a love-sick friend.

Her heart sighed unhappily for the young woman beside her. The early twenties were such a rotten time in a person's life, she commiserated, remembering her own passage into adulthood. And as Hannah had, Willie seemed determined to hold fast to her right to make her own mistakes and to muddle through her life her own way.

As sympathetic as she was to Willie's plight, she couldn't figure out how she'd gotten embroiled in Willie's ill-fated love affair.

Well, that wasn't quite true. She did know. And how could Hannah have refused to accompany Willie, when the girl thought she was doing her a favor by letting her tag along? She laughed softly at the silliness of it. But then, that was Willie too, a little silly.

Nine years earlier Hannah had moved into the

little house next door to the one shared by little Willie Willis and her mother, Dawn. It wasn't long before the twelve-year-old Willie had worn a path in the grass between the two back doors, coming and going in both houses as if she were the one paying the mortgages. Hannah had watched Willie grow into a lanky, wire-toothed teenager who was constantly at odds with her mother, and had seen her pass slowly into an extroverted, slightly off-the-wall young adult who had dreams and aspirations—to marry someone rich and exciting.

Yet, despite Hannah's reluctance to seize with enthusiasm the notion that marital bliss could be found on the road to rock 'n' roll stardom with a long-haired youth by the name of Randy Rendezvous, there wasn't anything she wouldn't do for Willie.

In her mind's eye, Willie would always be the little girl who had so readily and unpretentiously accepted Hannah into her heart with inordinate kindness and respect. No questions asked. No ifs, ands, or buts. To Willie, Hannah was simply Hannah. And for that reason alone, no favor was too great.

Not that the invitation to go would-be-superstar-and-potential-husband-gazing had been posed to Hannah as a favor, mind you. Willie was far too independent to need that kind of support. But she had been willing to let Hannah come along because she knew how much she loved to dance, and somewhere in the back of Willie's mind there was a synapse that had connected the loud, booming music at Flynn's with dancing.

From Hannah's point of view, however, it was a little more complicated.

It was one thing to dance in public with a male friend, and, while she might turn the volume of Willie's stereo up to a glass-shattering high and dance alone in private, it didn't mean the two forms of dance were interchangeable. She wouldn't think of dancing alone in public.

That left her with the options of dancing with Willie, an unlikely event in Willie's present state of mind, or dancing with a stranger, an idea that wasn't repugnant to her, merely implausible.

Hannah didn't feel . . . equipped, emotionally or otherwise, to strike up spur-of-the-moment conversations with strangers. She wasn't at her best with people she didn't know well, and therefore had a tendency to avoid personal contact with strangers whenever possible.

She did like people, though. They fascinated her. And she took every opportunity that came her way to throw herself into a happy horde of them. But a party animal? No. If Hannah were to classify herself as any type of social animal at all, it would have to be as an observer. The common garden variety, better known as a people-watcher.

She surveyed the mingling throng. There were men who were obviously looking for women; women looking for men; people who came simply to be with other people. Small groups celebrated being among friends. Solitary souls came to hide themselves in the crowd, while others came to stand out among the masses. There were those drinking to forget, and some sharing a night to remember. There were other people-watchers, waiters, and individuals like Hannah, who couldn't hold their feet still from the rhythm of the music.

She reached over and placed her palm on the metal railing that divided the table groupings from the dance floor. She could feel the beat of the music in the vibrations rising up into the metal through the floorboards. It was a light, fast-paced tempo that automatically made her ache to dance. She looked over at Willie and sighed, wishing the girl were a male rendition of her name, A William or a Bill.

A glance at her watch told her she had another half hour to endure the itch to dance without a partner, before Flynn's closed. She fought a momentary impulse to look back up at the man on the balcony and looked out in the opposite direction instead.

Hannah's gaze lifted slightly, passing over the heads of the bouncing mob to view the tranquillity of the ocean beyond. It was dark. The reflection of a full moon skipped across the water, became part of its eternal movement, and created a slow, sensual ballet of light in motion. Nothing in the immeasurable imagination of man could equal it.

But as beautiful as it was, Hannah couldn't appreciate it fully. Nighttime made her uncomfortable. She preferred daytime hours and well-lit places. Light was something she depended on to function. Friends teased her about being a solar unit, but the fact remained, darkness was not her friend. She never ventured into it unless someone was with her.

A hand came to rest on Hannah's shoulder. It was a calm, innocuous touch, but it startled her nonetheless. She turned in her seat and followed the trail from hand to face with her eyes.

The man from the balcony—definitely tall and infinitely better looking at close range—stood at her elbow. A small gasp stuck in her throat. Her heart lurched and sank slowly in her chest. It was her conclusion that there were strangers in one's life, and *then there were strangers*. Her stomach turned and was suddenly queasy. What she was feeling was not severe shyness, but a bad case of chronic caution.

She encountered many people in her career, and frequently made them friends. But there were those few newcomers in her life whom she very much wanted to meet and to make friends with, but who represented an enormous personal risk, and so much pain and humiliation that she was reluctant to approach them.

Such was the man from the balcony. She'd have given anything to be able to smile and flirt with him. The wide grin, the look of welcome in his eyes, and the lean, muscular body were all very tempting, but . . .

"Hi," he said, shouting to be heard over the music.

Hannah lifted her hand in greeting and watched his face intently, her smile uncertain. He glanced at Willie, who hadn't noticed him yet, and asked, "Is she dead or alive?"

Hannah couldn't help it; she laughed.

"I've been watching, and I don't think she knows you're here," he said, exaggerating his words so she could read his lips.

She nodded and conveyed that she agreed with that possibility.

"Would she miss you if I stole you away for a dance?"

Hannah frowned at him.

"Dance?" he bellowed.

His moustache made reading his lips difficult, but he was motioning toward the dance floor, and had a polite inquiry in his expression which helped Hannah to understand.

She wasn't sure if it was the way he was watching her, or if it was the curious churning sensation in her abdomen that kept her from accepting his offer immediately. He was like manna from heaven. An answer to her prayers for a dance partner. Still, she hesitated.

She knew what she was risking. She could imagine the look on his face when he discovered the truth about her. The shock. The disbelief. The wariness. She'd seen it before. And though she was wiser and more confident now, there was no denying that her childhood responses of shame, embarrassment, and subsequent anger lay just below the surface of the excited, giddy feelings he stirred in her.

But fortunately—or unfortunately, depending on the outcome—Hannah's middle name was Afraid. She wasn't exactly an optimist, and she couldn't honestly say that she believed in giving everyone the benefit of the doubt, but she was very accustomed to doing the things that frightened her most. It was almost like a game to her.

"Dance?" he yelled, mistaking her qualms for confusion.

She smiled, and turned to touch Willie gently on the arm. When she had her attention, she swung two dancing fingers across the palm of her hand and pointed to the stranger.

Willie looked over her shoulder and narrowed her bright blue eyes to scrutinize the man. She gave him a thorough once-over, glanced back at Hannah for an endorsement, then nodded her approval.

He looked as if he'd just won a prize. His fingers curled around Hannah's wrist before he turned and proceeded to part the sea of people between them and the dance floor. Amazingly, he did it with as much finesse as Moses at the Red Sea.

There was no pushing or shoving. The good-timers seemed to automatically take notice of him. They smiled, stepped aside, and alerted those with their backs to him to do the same. He nodded and continued to walk, unimpeded.

Hannah was feeling very strange. It was a little like she felt at the beginning of a long journey: Packed and ready to go, still unsure if all the details were taken care of, trying to remember if she'd unplugged the iron, hoping the plane wouldn't crash, wondering if her destination would live up to her expectations. And then, full of doubt and misgivings, fastening her seat belt and waiting for the plane to start moving.

Just as they stepped onto the dance area, the building stopped vibrating. The music stopped. The other dancers came to a slow halt, disentangling themselves from one another and dispersing.

Hannah knew a moment of panic as calm and quiet settled into her body. Would the man take the opportunity to speak to her? She watched the back of his head carefully, waiting for him to turn and say something.

They walked against the flow of people, which again seemed to separate magically in deference to the man from the balcony. There were smiles exchanged between him and the crowd. But it was the unrestrained stares that led her to suspect that he was no average customer of Flynn's.

She didn't have time to wonder who he was at the moment, however, for he turned toward her then, having come to the center of the dance floor. Again he smiled at her in a deep, appreciative manner. He was still holding her wrist as he glanced quickly over her body. Her skin warmed, and her heart fluttered in her chest. He was obviously pleased by what he saw as his gaze returned to hers.

"I can't believe I didn't have to fight someone for this dance," he said.

She didn't understand, but she smiled anyway. He was watching her every move, like a man on a fact-finding mission. Observing, gathering information. She couldn't take it. She'd been stared at before, but not the way he was staring at her. Not as if she were something wondrously special. She opened her mouth to speak just as the music began to pulsate through the room again.

He shot an annoyed glance at the band, but was laughing good-naturedly when he turned back to

Hannah. The vibrations of the music tickled the soles of Hannah's feet. She glanced at the other dancers.

The song was one of those with a slower beat, one that could be danced to in any fashion. The man slipped his arms around Hannah and chose to make it a slow dance. With her palms open on his chest near the ridge of his broad shoulders and his hands on her hips, they swayed to the slow, easy rhythm.

Hannah's senses were in turmoil. She still had the feeling that she knew him, but surely she'd recall having met a man who left her breathless and made her pulse skip about erratically. Several times she looked up, wondering what color his eyes were, wondering where they had met before. She'd forget to feel the rhythm of the music. She'd stumble. He'd smile and act as if it were a natural thing to do.

Maybe it was, she decided. Missing a beat here and there while dancing with someone for the first time wouldn't be such an outrageous thing to do. With that thought she began to relax a little.

Colt McKinnon wasn't at all relaxed. He was as jumpy as a frog in an anatomy lab. A hundred women had tucked their heads of soft curls under his chin and pressed their bodies close to his in dance, but they'd never made him feel as if he had ten thumbs and two left feet. They hadn't had large, light-colored eyes that were heavily fringed with dark lashes, or a gaze that seemed to travel through time and from far away places to reach out to him. They hadn't had full, pouty lips that were ever-ready for kissing, or skin as smooth and fresh as a baby's.

It was as if it were the first time; his first dance with a beautiful woman. He wasn't sure where to put his hands or what to say. He was being careful not to do anything to offend her or scare her away.

He was terrified that at any moment she might evaporate into thin air.

Hannah loved to dance. Her body had a natural aptitude for it. She could feel the cadence of the music in every fiber of her being. It filled her. And then her body simply took over and moved.

He said something. She was sure he had, because he was looking at her with an expectant expression. With her eyes, she asked him to repeat himself. He did. The music was blaring, so he spoke loudly and distinctly.

Again, Hannah frowned. She couldn't hear him, and she couldn't make out what he was saying because part of his mouth was covered by his moustache, and the fractured lighting threw shadows across it.

He leaned closer to repeat himself, and again Hannah frowned at him. She pointed to her ears and shook her head. She still couldn't hear him. What he had to say must have been important, because he took her by the arms and pulled her close. Close enough to scream into her ear.

His breath and the reverberation of his words tickled her neck, and she laughed, pulling away spontaneously. He laughed too, shook his head, and gave up trying to talk to her while the band was playing.

More and more, as they swayed in close proximity, she began to suspect that he was no ordinary man. While those in the crush around them were elbowed and bumped, they had plenty of room to move. It was as if he generated a force field that kept everyone but her at arm's length.

When he wasn't smiling, his was a pretty ordinary face. He had thick, dark hair that was clipped short on the sides. It wasn't excessively curly, but it had a body to it that made it look healthy and soft. His interfering moustache was the same, thick and clipped short. His profile was strong—

broad brow, straight nose, square jaw. She smiled as she noted his over-long eyelashes, a paradox to his strong, manly features.

He caught her grin and returned it. He beamed at her, light emanating from his eyes, illuminating his thoughts. She liked the animation in his face. It made speech almost unnecessary. She became warm all over as she realized that he was, once again, thinking her beautiful.

Speaking once more, he said in a magnified manner, "Do you live in Virginia Beach? Or are you vacationing?"

She frowned at him.

He pointed to the floor. "Do you live here?"

She nodded, and she cursed his moustache again. She hadn't understood what he'd asked her, but her affirmative answer had satisfied him.

They danced, communicating with smiles and eye contact that were as hot and searing as laser beams. There was a connection between them, a familiarity that went far beyond the few minutes they'd been dancing together. Their bodies seemed preacquainted, fitting together perfectly, as if they were two halves of a whole.

Hannah's head came to rest near his shoulder, and his arms circled her body as if they'd done so a thousand times before. She felt warm and safe close to his body. With her hand she could feel his heart beating under the smooth cotton of his shirt. It spoke to her in a language that was as old as time, yet still a mystery. It communicated its strength and loyalty. It told of pain and great joy. It revealed its needs and treasures.

They danced while their hearts spoke of dreams and the reality of a tomorrow. Their bodies cleaved, one to the other, as their hearts began to pound out tiny, fragile links in a chain that would bind their spirits together.

Hannah wasn't sure if she believed in love at

first sight, but she believed that this man would change a part of her forever. A part so deep inside of her that she hadn't been aware of its existence until the moment he had touched it.

She was alerted to the last beat of music when the other dancers stopped and began to move away. She sighed. She hated for the dance to end.

The man must have sensed her reluctance, or had some regret of his own, because he wouldn't release her when she tried to step away. Gently but insistently he pressed her head back to his shoulder and continued to dance. She felt a steady vibration in his throat against her cheek. He was humming the music. She smiled, liking the man's romantic nature, wallowing in the wonderful spell he was casting upon her.

When he again had control of her body and knew that she wouldn't try to leave him, he pulled away slightly to look at her face. He obviously enjoyed looking at her, but his gaze made Hannah a little nervous and jittery. He always seemed to be looking for something deep in her eyes—in her soul. He never appeared disappointed with what he saw; he merely kept trying to see more.

"Who are you?" he asked, a glimmer of wonder and awe in his voice as well as in his eyes.

Hannah could only smile, too enthralled to think.

He smiled back. "A mystery woman, huh?"

Of their own volition, her fingers traced the smooth angle of his cheek and jaw. She saw the difficulty he had swallowing and knew he was as enchanted and fascinated as she was.

"I'm Colt," he said.

She looked surprised, shook her head, then fanned her face with her fingers. "I'm hot," she said.

He chuckled.

"No. My name is Colt." He frowned up at the

band again as the room began to throb with music once more. He shouted, "Colt McKinnon."

With a finger to her ear she indicated that she hadn't heard him. He closed his eyes in frustration and hopelessness and placed his forehead to hers as if trying to communicate with her by mind fusion. His head came up and he searched the room with his eyes, finally lingering on the wall of glass that overlooked the ocean beyond.

He took her by the hand and led her away from the crowd to the window. The heat in the room and the cool air from the water and the late April night had formed a fine film of condensation on the window. In it he wrote his first name.

His name was Colt. She smiled. She liked it. It suited him. With one finger Hannah wrote her name below his. Then she looked at him and watched as her name appeared on his lips. He nodded, satisfied and pleased. He said it again as his gaze roamed over her face.

She watched him, mesmerized, not thinking or feeling, stunned by the moment. They could have been on the edge of the universe, one step from oblivion, and she would have remained fearless and trusting of the man before her.

She wasn't sure how she came to be in his arms or when she began to hope that he'd kiss her, but suddenly there she was, embraced and hoping like crazy. There was a small, reflective smile on his lips, a torrent of passion in his eyes as his face moved closer to hers. She grew dizzy with anticipation.

His mouth was soft and gentle at first, testing, experimenting, finding the best place to tarry and nibble. She leaned closer, plying her body to his, wanting more. His arms tightened about her, and he deepened the kiss. The tip of his tongue tapped lightly on her teeth, seeking entrance, and then slipped inside to make itself at home.

He tickled and teased, and her senses teetered and reeled out of balance. She *was* on the edge of the universe, and there *was* nothing else but Colt to cling to. An immense yearning collected in the core of her being.

They separated, but remained connected in a way that was more profound than words and more penetrating than touch. The fright and awe of what existed between them was plain to see in their expressions. So too was the joy and gladness. They both knew it was too huge, too powerful, and too quick to be handled with any degree of finesse or common sense. So they contented themselves with sharing a tiny space in time in which to marvel at and savor their emotions.

Wish, and it shall be so? Colt couldn't get over his good fortune, and was wondering what he'd done right lately. They were alone. No blaring band. No other people. And she was allowing him the pleasure of looking at her. That was all he'd wanted. Other delights danced in the back of his mind. Touching her, talking with her, hearing her laughter, listening to her moan with need and sigh with satisfaction. He wanted all those things too. He wanted to crawl inside of her and lose himself. But he wasn't a greedy man. One wish come true at a time was all he could hope for, and he counted himself lucky at that.

He reached out and touched the long dark curls at her shoulder, twisting them through his fingers as if they were something fine and fragile. The pad of his thumb brushed across her cheek. Quick, keen eyes that observed all that happened around her were focused on him—saw only him—and he wanted to keep it that way.

Her heart sat in her throat. She was breathing hard and fast. Tickling prickles washed across her skin, leaving her numb and excited at once.

She jumped at a sudden touch that wasn't his.

Colt frowned when she turned away from his arms to greet the fuzzy-haired blonde she'd been sitting with earlier. Hannah looked flustered and surprised to see her.

"I hate to break up a good thing," Willie said, smiling at each of them in turn, and truly repentant for the interruption, "But they're closing this place," she said with a sweeping gesture of her hand.

They both glanced around before their gazes met again. They laughed softly and sadly and with great uneasiness. Good-bye wasn't what they wanted to say to each other, yet anything else would have been just as awkward.

"Thank you for the dance," Hannah said finally. She felt she had many things to thank him for. The dance, the kiss, the touch. The expression on his face. "It was wonderful."

"Wait a second," he said, taking hold of her wrist. "Do you have to leave now? I mean, you don't have to if you don't want to. I . . . I own this place, and we could sit and talk awhile. Or maybe we could go somewhere else and talk."

"Talk?" she asked in a low, thick voice. "About what?"

Taken aback, he faltered. Hadn't she felt it? he wondered. Hadn't it affected her the way it had him?

"Just . . . talk," he said. "I don't even know your last name."

This was it, Hannah told herself. *That* moment. The moment of decision that led to the look of shocked disbelief, to the scowl of confusion, repulsion, pity, or rejection. The moment that she always dreaded with strangers. The moment when the apprehension and embarrassment that she kept so carefully under control rose up inside of her like a wild beast.

She stood looking at Colt, swaying between the

feelings of trust and safety she'd felt with him seconds earlier and the pain she'd experienced over and over again in the past.

Who was he anyway? she thought briefly. They were strangers to each other, and not likely to ever meet again. Couldn't she just walk away? Couldn't she keep the memory of the few minutes they had spent together as something special, something so out-of-this-world wonderful that nothing could tarnish it? Couldn't she just this once be spared *that look*?

In an instinctive instant of greed and self-protection she decided to snatch the memory and run.

Colt watched the beauty in her face crumble into despair. She lowered her eyes and turned to walk away from him.

"Hey. Wait a second," he said, reaching out to her again but missing his hold. "Wait. What's wrong?"

"Nothing's wrong," Willie said, always aware and always protective of Hannah, whether either of them noticed it or not. "She said the dance was wonderful."

Colt hardly noticed Willie, only the tone of her voice, which warned him not to pursue the issue. He watched Hannah walk quickly and determinedly away.

"I don't know your last name," he called. When she stopped at the table to retrieve her purse, he took several steps forward, saying, "I want to see you again."

She didn't even look at him.

"Her name is Alexander. Hannah Alexander," Willie said in a moment of pity for the man.

"Hannah? Did you hear me?" he asked, only half hearing Willie. "I want to see you again."

She turned from the table and started walking toward the exit.

What had he done wrong?

"Hannah." His voice echoed through the nearly empty nightclub. He called her name once more before she disappeared. Angry and frightened more than he ever believed possible that he'd never see her again, he started out after her. "Dammit to hell, what's the matter with her? Is she deaf or what?" he said.

At the edge of the dance floor he stopped cold as an eerie silence filtered into his consciousness. Slowly and with great trepidation, he turned back to Willie, who was following him at a leisurely pace.

She smiled at him in a friendly and understanding manner as she ambled to his side. Then she nodded and said, "Yes, as a matter of fact, she is deaf."

Two

"Did you forget to tell all these people that I'd be driving downtown today?" Hannah asked Willie facetiously, fighting to keep her temper and her concentration intact in the heavy traffic. She liked to drive, but the more traffic there was, the more there was to see and keep track of. It could be very draining at times. "Where do all these people come from?"

"Most of them pay me to let them come and watch you bash your way into a parking space," Willie said, leaning forward to sign as she spoke so Hannah could see what she was saying and find a parking space at the same time. "I told them you were in a bad mood. They probably think it'll be a better bash than usual."

"What are you talking about?" She frowned. Not at Willie, but because she'd driven around the same building three times without finding a parking place.

"You've been brooding over Mr. Virginia Beach for nearly two weeks now," Willie said, finger-spelling the words she didn't know signs for as Hannah watched her fingers peripherally. "You were two ships passing in the dark. It was a bump in the night. It happened and now it's over. Lighten up and forget it."

"I have not been brooding," Hannah said testily. "I have nothing to brood about. I'm going to be late for this meeting."

She made a quick motion with her hands when the car ahead of her pulled into the first empty parking space she'd seen all morning. It was one of the first signs Willie had learned, and her eyebrows rose knowingly. Concealing her emotions wasn't one of Hannah's strong points.

"As long as you're in a bad mood already, I may as well tell you that Peter called again," Willie commented lightly.

"What did he want?"

"Same old thing. He wants to know when you're going to show the rest of your work to Sheila Merritt."

"I told him I'd show her the rest of the pictures when I was ready. I'm not ready. Why won't he leave me alone?"

"He's your agent. You pay him not to leave you alone. And a show at the Merritt Gallery . . . well, it isn't something to spit at, you know."

She stopped the car in the traffic lane outside Gary Sherwin's office and turned to Willie.

"You park this stupid thing. I can only concentrate on one thing at a time. I want this job, and if I don't go now, the meeting will be over." She opened the door, grabbing her purse and portfolio from the back seat. "Sometimes I wish everyone would just leave me alone." Another complaint caught up with her. "And *if* I've been in a bad mood, it's because you keep telling me I'm in a bad mood and talking about ships and bumps and . . . If you weren't constantly talking about that man at the beach, I'd forget about him a whole lot faster."

She slammed the door closed, hurried between

two parked cars, up the steps, and through the thick glass doors of the building. Lord, she hated being late. Especially with new clients, when she wanted to make a good impression. She pushed both up buttons between the two sets of double elevators and began to tap her foot impatiently.

She couldn't bear to think of the impression she'd made on the man at the beach—with Colt, she thought dismally, remembering his name in a warm way. Running away like a coward. She called herself a few more choice names in anger and regretted that she'd never have an opportunity to redeem herself. He had been angry and upset when she'd left. Willie had told her. And he'd been even more so when he couldn't get her to give him more information about Hannah.

She sighed. It couldn't be changed now, she decided, glancing at her watch. Lord, she hated being late.

And she hadn't been brooding about him. She hardly ever thought about him . . . except at night . . . or during the day when she had nothing else to think about . . . or when she did have other things to think about but would suddenly remember and . . .

She glanced at her watch again and gave the up button several impatient jabs. She *really* hated being late.

Great photographers could get away with being late. They were said to have an artistic disposition. It wasn't merely being rude and unprofessional, it was considered eccentric and very much in character with the temperament.

Starving photographers could be forgiven a short period of tardiness, but they had to be appropriately apologetic.

But starving deaf photographers had misconceptions to dispel—even after they'd been offered a show at the Merritt Gallery. For some clients it seemed to follow that if a photographer couldn't hear they couldn't possibly take pictures.

Hannah always went out of her way to show herself in the best light to new clients. She was prompt and professional. As a person she had one tiny flaw; she was deaf. As a photographer, she had no flaws at all. If clients held the one flaw against her, it hurt. But it was their loss, their ignorance, and their unprofessionalism, not hers. . . . At least that was how she justified it and learned to live with it afterward.

She'd worn her favorite royal blue suit with a black silk scoop-necked blouse. She knew she looked great in it, and if she could manage to calm the nervous tremors in her hands, she could land the assignment. She had to. How hard could it be to photograph a race car driver anyway? she wondered. Gary had said something about a few location shots, but how tough could that be?

She glanced quickly around the empty lobby, then thrust her pelvis forward and slouched a bit to practice her limp I-hang-around-the-tracks-all-the-time stance while she waited for the elevator to appear. No problem, she decided, checking the numbers above the doors. One set was being held up on the eighteenth and fifteenth floors, the other on the ninth and tenth. She sighed.

Movement at the main entrance caught her attention, and she turned to complain to Willie about the slowness of the elevators. The words stuck in her throat. She felt as if everything but the chandelier was suddenly stuck in her throat when the man from the beach . . . the man from the balcony . . . when Colt walked through he doors.

He stopped when he saw her, recognizing her with the same instantaneous clarity. The night, the music, the dance. The feelings, the touch, the kiss . . .

Colt had been looking forward to seeing her again. He'd straightened his tie and smoothed back his hair seconds before entering the building. He just hadn't expected to see her standing in the lobby like an apparition from one of his dreams.

He'd spent a miserable two weeks trying to find her. He had prolonged his stay in Virginia Beach two extra days. All the information he'd been able to drag out of her friend was her name and occupation. Obsessed by the smell of her hair, haunted by the look in her eyes, and missing her smile, he'd called every Alexander in the phone book before it occurred to him that she'd have no need for a conventional telephone. After that he had gone to every photography studio in Virginia Beach asking if they knew of her.

Discouraged and plagued with regrets, he'd returned home and gone back to work, knowing that her memory would fade with time. But he was wrong. He began to feel possessed, as if she'd taken control of his mind. She was all he could think about. Day after day he'd thought of little else until, like a miracle, during a business call with his old friend Gary Sherwin, he'd taken a desperate, last-ditch stab in the dark and asked Gary if he'd ever heard of her.

Getting Gary to arrange the meeting had been easy. But seeing her again and knowing a little more about her, he started to wonder if maybe he shouldn't have put the memory of her in his pocket and saved it for nights when he needed something special and beautiful to think about. The reality of her didn't look easy at all. It looked fragile and not at all shatterproof.

He hesitated briefly, then walked slowly toward her. Their gazes locked. For an endless moment they stared at each other, remembering and want-

ing what they'd found the last time they'd met, not
knowing how to bring it back.

It was as if they'd had the same dream one night.
A wonderful, fantastic dream. But it hadn't been
real; it hadn't really happened; they weren't actually the people in the dream. . . . It was just a
fantasy. . . . And it was a damn shame. It seemed
all they could do was start over, pretend to be
strangers who'd met once briefly.

Hannah gave him a small smile of recognition,
which he returned with a softly spoken "Hi," which
she saw but couldn't hear.

"Hello," she said, still reeling from the sight of
him. Where had he come from? Was he really
there? Or was she playing make-believe again?

"Hi," he said again stupidly.

A nervous laugh escaped her. "Hello."

An inexplicable wave of relief washed over him.
He knew that she had spoken to him at the club,
he could remember every word she'd said. But he'd
been reading so many books about deafness lately
that whether or not she'd speak to him had had
him worried.

Self-conscious, they turned to watch the elevator
lights slowly descend by number.

Colt couldn't help it, he took another quick look
at her. At first he'd gone to the library to read
about deafness because he'd felt like an idiot. Why
hadn't he noticed that she was deaf? Several books
later he'd finally chalked it up to the music and the
fact that nobody *looks* deaf. It had been an easy
mistake for him to make.

That left him with the question of why she'd
reacted as she had, and why she hadn't wanted to
tell him. A little more reading had solved that
puzzle as well. Too risky for her. She tilted her
head, and he looked away.

Certainly no authority on deafness, he'd gleaned

enough information to realize that it was just as risky for a hearing person to try to broach the distance between sound and silence. Lifetimes of conditioning separated the two worlds with enough space to allow for every conceivable misunderstanding to take place in both spheres.

Silence was taken for stupidity or retardation. Independence was misconstrued as belligerence or emotional instability. Kindness and common courtesy were confused with pity, disdain, and condescension. Ignorance and a lack of understanding on both sides became pain, anger, resentment, and withdrawal, perpetuating the distance between the two environments.

He glanced at Hannah again and felt something hard and tight in his chest. Deaf or not, she was still the most beautiful woman he'd ever seen in his life. She looked at him then with those faraway eyes. They were green, he noticed—bright, clear, hazel green. She blinked away again, and he sighed.

Colt thought of himself as an ordinary man. Growing up in rural Virginia, he hadn't come across enough Spanish- or French-speaking people to warrant him learning a second language, nor had he ever planned to live abroad. Yet in his entire life he'd met more Spanish- and French-speaking people than he had deaf people. But he'd never once wished to know a second language more than he did at that moment—sign language.

One of the bells on the set of elevators behind them alerted them to its presence on the main floor. He turned and walked inside. Hannah continued to stand and watch the numbers above the elevators on the opposite wall.

Colt frowned. Wasn't she going up after all? Or didn't she want to get into the elevator with him? Was she angry? He probably should have said more to her. . . . He'd wanted to say more, but . . .

With a grimace he suddenly grasped that she hadn't heard the elevator arrive. With still another contorted expression, he pondered his situation. Should he draw her attention to the available elevator? Would that make her feel foolish or stupid? Or would it be the most natural thing to do if one person knew the other person was deaf and hadn't heard the bell?

It was very confusing for him. He wouldn't hurt her for the world, and he certainly didn't want to make her feel any more awkward. On the other hand, he didn't want to disregard the fact that she was deaf, or pretend that she wasn't.

Impulsively, he pressed the tenth button on the inside panel, tiptoed quietly out of the elevator, waited for the doors to close again, and then quickly repushed the up button. He'd go back to the library and find out what he should have done, but for the moment the easy way out seemed best.

When Hannah turned and glanced at him again, he pressed the button a couple more times, saying, "Slow elevators."

She nodded innocently and smiled in agreement.

He nodded also, taking one giant step forward as he racked his brain for something to say to keep the conversation going.

"Nice weather, huh?" he asked, feeling like the world's biggest dolt.

"I'm sorry?"

He knew he was supposed to look directly at her and speak as normally as possible. Slower, maybe, so she could read his lips. He repeated himself, pointing to the main entrance and the bright sunshine beyond.

"Great May weather," she agreed.

Three whole words. Colt latched onto them and held them close. They were terrific words. She spoke well, in a deep, throaty monotone that was actually sort of sexy, he thought. And it wasn't at all hard to understand her if he listened closely. As a matter of fact, she didn't sound any more speech-impaired than someone with a thick foreign accent . . . or a bit of a cold in their nose.

An elevator they could both see arrived, and they walked in together. Colt was so thrilled at being able to communicate with her that he wanted to do it some more.

"Are you here on business?" he asked, wanting their meeting to seem like a coincidence.

When she didn't answer, he glanced at her and immediately realized his error. She was busy punching her floor number and waiting for the elevator to move. The curve of her waist, the small of her back, and her tight little tush were incredible, he noticed.

Moving to catch her attention, he motioned to her portfolio and waited for her to look at him before he repeated his question. "Are you here on business?"

Stupid darn moustache, she cursed inwardly when it hid all his words but "business." She took a gamble on his question. "I'm a photographer."

He nodded. "You live in Richmond, then." He knew she did, because Gary had told him.

What about Richmond? She lived there, worked there, did everything there—she supposed her answer would have to be, "Yes."

"That's great. At the beach I thought that you said you lived there, but . . . I live here too." He broke out in a cold sweat wondering if he should go further. "Maybe . . . maybe we could have dinner sometime."

Shew! He'd said a lot of words that time, and even the best lip readers couldn't catch *every single word*, and the accursed moustache was cutting her visibility by half. Great . . . beach . . .

you . . . here . . . maybe . . . sometime, didn't make any sense to her, but she didn't want him to stop talking.

"You never can tell," she said with a small smile. "It really is a small world, and people run into each other at the oddest times."

Colt nodded and smiled back, even as he began to suspect that he was doing something wrong.

Hannah's stomach tied itself into a tight knot when he looked away to stare at the elevator doors. She'd answered wrong. She knew she had. Here was her chance to redeem herself, and she'd blown it. Great impression she was making, huh? If he should happen to ask her out, she'd probably tell him she'd never been a girl scout. Why words? Why couldn't people simply exchange thoughts instead of words? Why did everything have to be so complicated?

She was such a jerk, she told herself. Why would a handsome man want to go out with a deaf person when he could have any number of beautiful hearing women? A familiar anger and resentment began to churn deep within her. Why the hell not? She was good enough to dance with in Virginia Beach. She was good enough to kiss. He thought she was beautiful that night. But now she's deaf, so she's not anymore?

She ground her teeth and seethed unreasonably in silence. It startled her when he suddenly turned toward her and threw his hands to his chest.

"Have dinner with me," he said, stooping to exaggerated lip movements.

She stared at him as the elevator opened, and let all her anger and hurt escape through the doors. She took a deep breath to try and control the irregular beating of her heart. There had been a one-in-a-million chance—one-in-a-trillion chance—of ever seeing him again after the once-in-a-lifetime night they'd shared. Fate had been the answer to many of the questions she'd had about her life so far. Things simply happened and were the way they were. Fate seemed to be taking a turn for the better.

A slight nod was all she could manage, letting the expression on her face show her acceptance of his invitation. His smile, with the glee-filled dimples and the light in his eyes that came from his soul, made her knees weak as she stepped out of the elevator.

"I'm sorry about . . . well, about leaving the way I did at the beach. It was rude," she said, blurting the words out. "I just . . ."

"It's okay," he said, shaking his head, still smiling. He'd have forgiven her anything to see her smile again. "Really. I understand."

Self-conscious and not knowing how to get to her meeting and prolong her encounter at the same time, she pointed down the hall to the doors of Gary Sherwin's public relations firm, indicating that it was her destination.

"What a coincidence," he said, looking pleasantly surprised. Then he pointed to her portfolio and asked, "Are you working with Gary?"

"Yes. I do a lot of work for Gary."

The receptionist placed her index and middle finger like a gun with no trigger to the outside corner of her eye, smiled fondly at Hannah, and said, "Hi, Hannah," before she turned a more professional smile to Colt and said, "Good morning, Mr. McKinnon, it's nice to see you again."

"Thanks. Gary been treating you right?" he asked, enjoying her blush of discomfort as she recalled that he had several times offered to steal her away from Sherwin.

"Yes, of course, and you can go right in. Mr. Sherwin's been waiting for you." He gave Hannah a see-you-later smile for good measure as he walked past her, and smirked when he heard the receptionist add, "Hannah, you can go in now too."

Gary was great, Colt decided. Their meeting was supposed to look like an accident, but he'd obviously come up with a better plan. Colt lifted his eyebrows in surprise and held the door open for her. He took his time, watching as Hannah walked confidently into the office. "Hello, Gary," she said.

"Hannah. There you are. . . . Oh, and you've met Colt already," the short, wiry man said as he skirted the end of his desk to plant a kiss on her cheek. "Colt," he said, extending a hand in friendship and winking conspiratorially. "It's good to see you again."

Hannah seated herself while the two men shook hands. She always sat in the same chair. The one that faced both Gary's desk chair and the two extra chairs in front, with her back to the window so the sun wouldn't be in her eyes.

They exchanged a few words before Gary moved back behind his desk and began to speak both verbally and with his hands. Colt noted that being bilingual seemed to be second nature to Gary, and couldn't help being envious of his ability to communicate with Hannah so easily. He'd known Gary for years on a friendly as well as professional basis. Why hadn't his knowledge of sign language ever come up in a conversation?

"Have the two of you been introduced properly?" he asked, pretending to assume that they hadn't been. "Hannah Alexander, meet Colt McKinnon."

They smiled shyly at each other, nodded politely, then waited for Gary to wave a wand or cast a magic spell—to do something that would make things right and easy between them.

"Hannah, I'm especially glad that you could make it to this meeting," he said. "It was short notice, but once the idea came to me, I . . . well, this will be incredible." He shifted his weight with excitement, and then launched into his explanation. "Colt here wants a full-length promotional brochure done on his NASCAR team and the cars they're racing this year and building to race next year. It's a fabulous opportunity for your— What's wrong?"

Hannah was confused. "I thought . . . Willie said you owned the nightclub at the beach," she said, looking at Colt, not sure how she felt about him being the racer she was supposed to photograph.

"I own a race car, too," he said, a bit preoccupied. He wasn't sure what his publicity brochure had to do with Hannah's being there, but if Gary was thinking what Colt thought he was thinking . . .

"Colt's team is going to win the Winston Cup next year," he boasted, grinning at Colt. "Big races, big bucks, big names, and big publicity. And Hannah, I think you're just the girl we need to get the big photo shots we need for this campaign."

"Ah, Gary?" Colt broke in, floored by what he was hearing. He glanced quickly at Hannah and back again to Gary. "Were—are you planning to have Hannah do the pictures for the brochure?"

Gary's eyebrows rose upward toward his bald head, his blue eyes looking askance. "Yes I was. It was a stroke of brilliance on my part, even if I do say so myself. But . . ." He looked from one of them to the other. "Why? Is there a problem?"

Hell yes, there was a problem. Colt had a fistful of problems with the idea of Hannah handling the photography he'd had in mind and already discussed with Gary for his new brochure. And not once had Hannah's name entered into the scheme of things professionally. Studio work wasn't at all what he'd been planning on, and if Gary thought . . .

"Well, I thought we'd discussed having a lot of

location shots," Colt said as tactfully as he possibly could. "We took second place at Daytona. My brother, Trevor, is doing really well this year in the Grand Nationals, and it would be a good time to show off the team's records and . . . well, I thought the sponsors might like to see a few shots of the winners' circle this year, and then there are the cars and the promo stuff for the Winston Cup next year . . ."

"Location shots are no problem, are they, Hannah?" Gary asked. "It would be racetracks, garages." He chuckled. "Greasy places like that?"

"No problem," she said, smiling at both men. She could see that Colt was having some difficulty dealing with the idea of a woman photographer handling a shoot at a primarily male sporting event, but she'd done it before, and she could do it again.

No problem? He looked at Hannah as if she'd lost her mind. Colt was fast falling head over heels in love with her, but he was still a businessman. He wanted track shots and action photos, not pictures taken from the stands with long-range or telephoto lenses. And if she was thinking . . . oh, Lord, if she was even contemplating the thought of going down on the field with her cameras . . .

She was deaf, for crying out loud. Racetracks were dangerous enough—even for people with excellent hearing. They'd be death traps for her.

"I don't know, Gary," he said, rubbing the back of his neck as he avoided eye contact with Hannah. "Do you think this is a wise decision? I mean, for Hannah."

"What did you say? I missed that," Hannah asked, turning quickly to Gary when Colt began to hide his words and expressions from her. She could see that he was still having doubts about her, but she was beginning to feel that her gender wasn't the problem after all.

Gary turned to her and spoke, again using small hand gestures to help her understand. "Colt's wondering if you are the wisest choice for this job. He—"

"Why?" she broke in, her normal defense shields locking automatically into place as she looked at Colt. "Because I'm a woman?"

Oh, please, say that's the reason, Colt. Please, she prayed. Defending womanhood was so much easier to handle than trying to defend being deaf.

"Well, that's one reason," he said.

"I'm sorry?"

Gary interpreted for her. She wanted everything Colt said to be made perfectly clear to her. His moustache made reading his lips especially difficult, and there was no room for guesswork anymore.

"What's the other reason?" she asked point-blank, already knowing the answer and growing angrier by the minute.

Colt stood up and turned his back on her as he began to pace. If he told her he didn't want her professionally because she was deaf, he was dead in the water with her personally. He knew that. But he wanted to be completely honest with her, no matter what kind of relationship they had.

"The tracks are dangerous under the best of conditions, Hannah," he said, looking at her as he spoke, aware that Gary was signing for her as her eyes darted between the two of them. "It's a rough sport." He bolstered his courage and then spit out the words, "I think your deafness would be a problem. A big problem."

"Why?"

"Why?" His look was incredulous. "Because you wouldn't be able to hear anything."

"What do I need to hear to take pictures of race cars?"

That stumped him. He knew she would be extra

careful with her eyes, he'd seen how aware of her surroundings she could be. But he also knew that many things got by her—elevators, for instance.

"Hannah, really, I don't mean to offend you, but it's dangerous," he said, specific instances failing him. "It would be like blindfolding you and standing you on the edge of a cliff."

Gary finished interpreting, and then burst out laughing as a defiant and very cheeky smirk rippled across Hannah's lips.

"What?" Colt was perplexed and feeling very uneasy.

Gary made a half-hearted effort to control his mirth, but found it difficult. Finally he said, "Remember those shots of Buzz Elliot you liked so much? A couple of years ago? The ones on my office wall at home?" He waited for Colt's affirmative answer. "Hannah took them."

"Oh no." Colt groaned, reaching for the back of the chair and lowering himself into it.

He could feel the blood draining out of his face as he recalled the photos he'd seen of Buzz Elliot, a world-renowned mountain climber, rappelling off a straight-faced crag of rock miles above a ragged ravine. Nausea gripped him as he brought forth the images of elation in the man's eyes, the pride and determination in the grim set of his jaw, and the beads of sweat on his brow—knowing that the pictures couldn't have been taken other than at close range.

The vision of Hannah, hanging from those rocks with a sliver of a rope between her and the ravine . . . well, it made him physically weak, but it also made him want to scream. He had an instant, insane urge to kill both Buzz Elliot and Gary for allowing her to do such a thing—and to strangle her for doing it.

"You took those pictures of Buzz Elliot?" he asked, his controlled voice an indication of his wrath, though she wasn't aware of it. "You climbed that mountain and took those pictures?"

"Yes," she said, liking the look of disbelief and terror on his face.

"And you let her?" Colt growled at Gary, his jaw twitching with rage.

The older man shrugged helplessly. "She took those shots before I knew her. They were her calling card to me . . . through my sister. They went to school together."

Hannah had missed the exchange between the men, as she'd gotten up in preparation to do battle with Colt.

"Mr. Elliot was pleased with my work, Mr. McKinnon," she said, pronouncing his last name "McKinnin." If he wanted to think that she labored alongside the famous mountain climber to get her shots, she wasn't about to inform him of the truth at this point, she decided. There were secrets to every trade, and she could see she was going to need the edge to get the job. "I see no reason why you wouldn't be just as pleased with my efforts."

He wanted to jump up and shake some sense into her. "I have no doubts at all about your talent, Hannah," he said instead. "That was never at issue."

The office door opened, and they all turned to look as Willie entered the room, pushing her wild bush of blond curls away from her freckled face.

"Sorry I'm late," she said quietly, closing the door. "I had to park four blocks away." When she noticed everyone staring at her in an overheated state, she smiled self-consciously and added, "It's really warming up out there. Oh, look," she exclaimed, suddenly surprised. "It's you from the beach."

Willie was a far cry from the professional interpreters Hannah had used on occasion. She didn't adhere to any code of ethics but her own, but her services were cheap for the asking, and as her friend and photo assistant, she came in handy during business discussions.

Colt gave her a nod and a half-smile of recognition, but it was Hannah who spoke next.

"You remember Mr. McKinnon, don't you, Willie? It turns out that he's the client Gary wanted us to meet. But he doesn't seem to think I can handle the job."

Willie bobbed her head with great understanding, then turned to take a chair, muttering, "Uh-oh," under her breath.

Hannah looked back to Colt. "If it's not my photography or my sex that's bothering you, then my deafness is your greatest objection. Is that right, Mr. McKinnon?" she stated, speaking as calmly as her irritation would allow. "Would it help to know that Willie is not only my friend and assistant, but that she is also a very good interpreter?"

"Well, that helps, but . . ."

"Or is it my speech? You don't think I'll be able to make myself understood. Is that it?" she asked, more than a little disheartened. She'd been told that she spoke very well. It hurt terribly to know that he found her difficult to understand, or even worse, that her voice irritated him.

"Now that's got nothing to do with it. I—"

"All right, Mr. McKinnon," she jumped in again, pained, angry, and close to desperate for the job. "I'll tell you what I'll do. I'll take a photo session anywhere you choose, for free. I won't talk in your presence if it irritates you. I'll have Willie interpret everything for me, even though I do read lips better when people have two lips instead of just one. But if that's the way it has to be, it will be. And if I don't give you great pictures, you can . . ." What? she mused briefly in her fury. What was the worst thing he could do to her—other than reject her completely? "You can have my favorite Nikon."

Whoa! Was that an offer he wasn't supposed to be able to refuse? he wondered, wanting to laugh suddenly. She couldn't have bet her body? Or at least a kiss? He chewed on his lower lip to keep from insulting her once again.

He'd made a royal mess of things so far, but to tell the truth, he wouldn't have missed this show of subdued temper and overpowering spirit for the world. Good lord, if he'd been falling in love with her before, he was stone cold, flat out *in* love with her now, he thought.

His fears for her safety notwithstanding, and realizing that she wasn't going to welcome any protection he tried to offer her after he'd put her on the defensive, he simply didn't know how he could refuse her.

Hannah stood her ground, even though she could feel tears threatening to squeeze through their ducts to embarrass her. His expression was gravely serious, and she could almost feel his refusal like a knife in her abdomen. When he finally frowned deeply and began to speak, she braced herself against the back of the tall leather chair.

His moustache got in the way of his words once again, and she looked to both Gary and Willie for help.

Gary spoke first, "He wants to know what you meant about one-lipped people." Then he laughed, as if he'd heard the joke before.

"I realize that I can be difficult to understand when I speak, Mr. McKinnon, but it's also very hard for me to understand you, because you only have one lip."

"What?" Involuntarily his fingers moved to count his lips.

"When a man wears a moustache, it's as if he

only has one lip. I can lip-read much better when there are two."

He averted his eyes to hide his amusement, and when he thought he could handle himself properly, he pushed himself out of the chair and walked across the room to her.

"First I want to make a couple of things very clear," he said, sure that he had her attention. "You speak well. I don't have any trouble understanding your words, and I do not find your voice offensive. Okay? Did you get all that?"

"Yes," she said, victory warming her heart as she felt the tides turning in her favor.

"As to your proposal for the free photo session, I'll take it," he continued. "And I will take your favorite Nikon if I don't like the pictures, so they'd better be good." He paused to make sure he was getting through to her, then, hoping to make one tiny stitch in the rift between them, he added, "But there is one condition."

"What?" she asked, suspicious and wary and still angry that she'd had to practically beg him to give her a chance.

"You have to call me Colt."

She weighed the condition and finally agreed. "I accept your condition, Mr. McKinnon. When I do the shoot, I'll call you Colt."

Colt inhaled deeply and stepped away from her. He felt defeated and resigned to the fact that he'd blown away any chance he'd had of building a relationship with Hannah through his own stupidity. He hadn't meant to, but he had. He'd watched her attraction to him wither and die before his eyes. And he'd destroyed it by adding insult to injury nearly every time he opened his mouth.

He spent what was left of their meeting with Gary Sherwin kicking himself and calling himself every conceivable type of fool while Hannah and

Gary exchanged news of Gary's sister. She apparently was also deaf—which finally explained his fluent second language and again left Colt feeling cheated and left out somehow.

And Hannah? Well, she was busy redefining the word disappointment. Colt McKinnon wasn't the hero she'd been waiting for all her life. He wasn't even the white knight she'd believed him to be the night they'd first met. She'd spent two weeks thinking—or to use Willie's term, brooding—about him, remembering the way he'd charged into her life, swept her off her feet, and carried her off to a place of enchantment and peace and beauty. It made her heart ache to discover that he was just one of those good old-fashioned fools who came a dime a dozen on nearly every street corner in the world, who thought handicapped meant nonfunctional. She was almost glad when he finally stood and took his leave.

Three

It was with a heavy heart that Colt left Gary Sherwin's office that day. He got as far as the main entrance on the first floor before he felt sufficiently bruised and battered with self-inflicted injuries to start thinking rationally again.

He was only going to get one chance with Hannah, and even though he'd gotten off on the wrong foot, it didn't necessarily mean that it was over, did it?

He knew failure. He'd met it once briefly a few years earlier, and he still woke up in the middle of the night with its grip squeezing life from his lungs. Until he'd met failure, he'd thought that nothing was out of his reach. He had money, power, prestige; everything he wanted. But failure hadn't taken away the things he'd wanted. No. It was a clever demon. As if draining the blood from his veins, it took what he *needed* to give his life meaning.

He knew failure. He recognized his failure with Hannah. He didn't just want her. There was something inside her that he needed. If he walked away from his one chance with Hannah, he knew it would choke the life from his spirit and haunt him for the rest of his days.

He walked briskly back to the elevators. This time it wasn't too late to fight failure. He wasn't going to allow it to take Hannah from him.

He felt an urge to get out and push the elevator as it moved slowly up to the fourteenth floor. He sprinted down the hall to Gary Sherwin's office but didn't bother to go all the way in.

"Has Hannah left?" he asked from the doorway.

"You must have missed her coming up, Mr. McKinnon. She . . ."

He didn't wait for the receptionist to finish, and when the elevators proved to be taking too long for him again, he ran around the corner to make use of the stairwell. Fourteen flights of stairs and as many silent prayers later, he burst through the glass doors onto the busy sidewalk. There was no sign of Hannah.

No, wait. The floppy mop of blond curls on Willie's head was across the street and half a block up. Hannah was beside her. Flowers seemed to bloom in his heart as he jogged across the street against the light and closed the distance between them—the physical distance anyway. He still had an emotional and intellectual schism to bridge, with no idea of how to go about it.

"Hannah," he called, still several yards behind them. "Hannah."

Needless to say, Hannah didn't hear him. But Willie did, and she turned, stopped, and then touched Hannah's arm to alert her to his presence.

A pained expression crossed her face when she saw him. He'd hurt her and made her angry. The tight bands of bitterness and frustration that were constricting her heart snapped loose at the sight of him, shooting pangs of a sweeter, deeper pain through her chest. Profound gladness warred with a lifetime of caution.

Torn, she appealed to her pride and the survival instincts she'd honed over the years for support. She continued to walk away from him.

He darted past Willie to catch up with her, and finally, finally he was close enough to reach out and stop her.

"Hannah. Please," he said, panting for air. "I have to talk to you. I need . . . dammit." He closed his eyes and fought for command over his body and his emotions.

What he had to say was too important to be left to chance. He couldn't permit any more gross misunderstandings to come between them.

He looked into her eyes and knew he was right. Anything worth his love was worth a fight.

He looked back at Willie and swallowed what was left of his ego. He held his hands out plaintively. "I need your help. I need to be sure that she understands me."

Willie loved love. Romance was even better. She grinned and stepped closer. "Shoot," she said. "I'm at your service."

Hannah waited. He held her firmly but gently by the upper arms and shifted his weight nervously. The tremors in his hands shook through her body, passing on his tension and urgency. He looked first to Willie, then back at Hannah with fear and hope in his eyes.

"I'm sorry, Hannah," he spouted out abruptly. "I blew it. I made a mess of everything back there, and it was the last thing in the world I wanted to do." He paused to let Willie catch up. "The thing with Buzz Elliot? Hell, I wouldn't care if it was my worst enemy hanging off those rocks with him, I still would have thought it was crazy. I think Buzz is crazy. But with you . . . with you up there, it scared the hell out of me. I kept thinking, what if you'd died trying to get those pictures? What if I'd never gotten the chance to meet you? And it's not because you're deaf. It's because you're mortal. You are mortal, aren't you?"

He waited for Willie's hands to stop moving and then looked back at Hannah. She nodded.

"Good." He smiled. "Then try to understand that my only concern—*my only concern*—about you working on this project for me is your life. Too many things could happen to you. Hell, I don't even let my own mother go to the tracks unless there's someone around to take care of her. She's safer watching the races on T.V."

Hannah gave a negative shake of her head.

"What?" he asked.

"Do hearing women go to the races?"

"Yes."

"Do any of them ever go down to the pits and take pictures?"

He knew what she was getting at and considered lying to her.

"Tell the truth," she said, watching him closely.

"Yes."

"Then I will too."

"But it's different for you. You won't be able to hear the cars, and . . ."

Hannah turned and started to walk away again. As handsome as he was, as wonderful as he made her feel inside, it was plain to see that he wasn't really listening to her. And if he couldn't or wouldn't hear her now, he never would.

"Hannah, wait," he said. "Be reasonable. I'd feel responsible if anything happened to you, and—" he suddenly realized that he was arguing with himself. She had very effectively ended the discussion by turning her back on him.

He stepped forward and took her arm, turning her around.

"Fight fair," he said.

"If hearing women can go to racetracks, I can go to racetracks," she said flatly.

He stood back and looked at her, as if for the first time. He found it hard to swallow, and his chest felt full and stiff. He wanted to protect her, not from everything, certainly, but at least from the obvious dangers in life. Yet it was clear that she wasn't going to let him. He was going to have to let her go, let her do what she had to do, let her scare the holy living beegeebees out of him in order to keep her.

"Hannah, I'm driving in the dark without lights here. I don't know what I'm doing. Ignorance is a lousy excuse for anything, but it's the only one I've got. I don't know how to talk to you, or what I should say if I could. But I want to learn. I want to know you." His eyes were pleading. "Teach me. Teach me how to say I'm sorry."

Hannah had the distinct impression that "I'm sorry" wasn't something Colt had to say very often. "Excuse me," "pardon me," maybe an "oops" once in a while, but not "I'm sorry." And it wasn't because he was cold or callous. She had a feeling that he went to considerable trouble not to do things that he'd have to apologize for. What he'd done in Gary's office had come naturally to him. He hadn't meant to hurt or insult her, only protect her—as he would any woman, deaf or not.

Her ruling came clear and swift. She would be his teacher. She would be everything to him in time, she hoped. But the first lesson he was going to have to learn was that there wasn't enough cotton in the entire world to protect a deaf person. Every time they closed their eyes or moved deeply into thought, they lost the constant awareness of their surroundings and were in danger. But they had to take their chances with life and death just like everybody else . . . or they were the same as dead.

She held the little finger of her right hand in the air, placed it at the center of her chest, then closed her hand to a fist and made a clockwise circular motion over her heart. "This is how to say 'I'm sorry.' And this"—she placed the two-fingered gun at the corner of her eye as the receptionist in Gary's office had done, then touched both fingers to the palm of her left hand—"is my name."

A slow grin spread across his face, calling forth the playful dimples in his cheeks and the delight in his eyes. He looked like the man from Virginia Beach, confident, charming, and pleased by the sight of her. Well, maybe he wasn't the same man, maybe he was a better man.

He repeated her motions out of order as he spoke. "Hannah. I'm sorry." He fed himself some imaginary food, and asked, "Will you have dinner with me?"

She shook her head patiently, then shook the invisible spoon from his hand. "This is the sign for food," she said, pulling her poised fingers away from her lips. "For breakfast, lunch, or dinner. And this"—she touched her first two fingers to her thumb in a sharp motion—"is no."

"No? Why not?"

"I have other plans," she said. She didn't, but female coquetry isn't something a woman learns or practices with her ears.

He frowned and started muttering. She placed a hand on his arm and looked to Willie for assistance.

He shook his head. "You didn't miss anything. I was trying to figure out when we could see each other again," he said, smiling. "We race in Rougemont this weekend—"

"Hold it," Willie interrupted. "How do you spell that?"

"I don't know. Tell her it's a race in North Carolina." He looked back to Hannah and continued. "But there's two weeks between the Winston and the Coca-Cola, and we could . . ." Hannah was frowning. "What?"

"There's two weeks between cigarettes and a soft drink?"

He chuckled, his eyes twinkling merrily. "No. Those are races sponsored by those companies, in different towns."

"I see."

"Anyway, I could come get you one day next week and take you down to Roanoke. We're building a car there that will blow your mind," he explained. "And then maybe we could go to one of the smaller tracks so you can get a feel for what you'll be facing in Loudon the weekend after that. How does that sound?"

"It sounds fine, but I could drive myself."

He held his hands up defensively. "I know that. And if you really want to, that's fine. I was just thinking that since I had to go anyway and that we'd probably spend the night, we could go together . . . save gas. That's all."

"Spend the night?" she asked.

"Well," he said, choosing his words carefully. "It's a two-hour drive. There's a lot to see. There's a small dirt track near there that we could go to the next day. We . . . my family owns a farmhouse down there that has plenty of room. And you'll be bringing . . . ah . . ."—he looked at Willie—"Willie, right?"

"Right," Willie said. "Funny how intimate we've gotten here without a proper introduction." She sent a pointed look to Hannah. "I'm Willie Willis."

"Willie Willis?" He was caught off guard. "Really? That's your name?"

"Yes." She looked surprised that he was surprised, but she was actually quite used to the reaction.

"Fibber," Hannah whispered loudly, grinning ear to ear.

Willie's head went up indignantly. "I have an-, other name, but if you want me to continue inter- preting for you, and if you ever want to be my friend, you'll forget that and call me Willie."

"Fair enough," he agreed, having been saddled with Colton since birth. To Hannah he asked, "So what do you think? I'll pick you both up on Tuesday, take you to Roanoke, and bring you back Wednesday . . . or Thursday if you want to stay longer."

"Okay." She smiled, but the smile in her heart was ten times larger. "But do you realize that you're talking as if I'll be shooting the whole layout?"

"Yes."

"Are you sure that's what you want?"

"Positive."

"Because you feel sorry for me?"

"For crying out loud, Hannah," he said, mildly frustrated. "After what I've just been through, I *should* feel a whole lot sorrier for myself than I do for you."

"But you don't?" she asked, looking from Willie's fingers into his eyes, searching for doubts and pity, and finding none.

"No, I don't," he said firmly. "I'm going to go insane while I try not to worry about you at the track. But you're going to get me some great photographs. And that's what I want. . . . Well, it's one of the things I want from you," he amended.

His answer satisfied her, and intrigued her.

"I know the other thing you want from me," she said, flashing him a wily and provocative look through her dark fringe of lashes.

He glanced at Willie in a fluster, preferring to do his more intimate romancing without an audi- ence. But he was too tempted by her innuendo to shy away. His eyebrows shot upward in interest, and he shifted his weight expectantly. "I'll bet you do. But just so we're both clear on this point, you'd better tell me what else it is that you think I want from you."

Along with her many other talents Hannah also had terrific timing. She waited until he started to grow tense with his own imaginings, then said, "You want my favorite Nikon."

He stared at her for a long instant before he saw the laughter in her eyes.

"You're not the sweet little angel I thought you were, Hannah," he said, looking more fascinated than disappointed.

"I'm not a lot of things you thought I was, Colt," she reminded him, thinking that even though she'd tricked him, his carnal thoughts hadn't been too far off base.

He nodded, looking at her in yet another new light. She resembled the woman with the killer body, the honey-sweet lips, and the faraway eyes who had bedazzled him one night at a nightclub in Virginia Beach. She looked a lot like the beautiful deaf woman who'd taken control of his mind in the weeks that had followed. She was still the woman he'd fallen in love with in Gary Sherwin's office, and he still wanted to care for her and protect her as much as she'd let him.

But standing before him was also a woman with a thousand secrets he knew nothing about. A woman with her own dreams and ideas. With thoughts and opinions and skills and talents she had yet to reveal to him. Hannah was the woman he'd been waiting all his life to meet.

"If you two have your plans all settled," Willie said, breaking in on their silent tête-à-tête, "I'd like to hear about this brother of yours. He races, you said. Is he married? Tell me what . . ."

Four

"You're nuts," Trevor said, following his brother through the crowd at the small Durham airport. He hadn't removed his dark glasses, as the Carolina sun seemed as blinding indoors as it was out, and he still had a bit of a tension headache. A couple of beers to celebrate their second-place position at the track and a soft warm body to hang on his every word would be his cure. . . . Would be, that is, if Colt would let him get to them. "You really are nuts. You know that, don't you?"

"Yes." Colt didn't slacken his pace to answer. He was in a hurry.

Trevor grumbled under his breath. "You couldn't have taken an early plane tomorrow, I suppose."

"No."

Contrary to popular opinion, Trevor thought that on Saturday no man should have to do anything he didn't want to do. On Saturdays Trevor raced and wooed his women. He lived for Saturdays.

"And you couldn't have rousted Frank or Jerry out of the bar to drive you to the airport. It had to be me, right?"

"Right." Colt rolled his eyes heavenward.

The ride from Rougemont to Durham had taken at least a half hour, and he'd barely had time to shower after the race. If he didn't get back soon, all the cute girls would be taken. "This babe better be worth all this trouble, brother."

"She is."

Trevor was silent, but only long enough to rubberneck at a tall, lanky redhead.

"I still can't see where a day could make that much difference," he complained, hanging limply on the ticket counter while Colt bought his ticket and all but ignored him.

Through the strain of his headache came a small ray of opportunity, and his lips quirked with amusement as he watched his older brother drum his fingers impatiently. He didn't know why he was surprised that Colt was leaving early instead of flying back with him and the crew the next day. He hadn't been with them since they'd arrived in Rougemont on Thursday anyway. Not really. His body was there, getting in the way and wandering off, but they'd practically had to kick him every time they'd wanted his attention.

"Girls like to be kept in suspense, you know," Trevor said in a quiet, all-knowing manner, looking to have some fun with his brother.

Colt looked down his nose at his brother, who was slightly over six feet but still shorter than he was, and stared at him with a torpid expression. "Is that right?" he said.

"Yep. You've got to keep them guessing, and you don't want to look too eager to be with 'em, or they'll walk all over ya."

Colt took his ticket from the attendant, thanked her, and walked away, knowing Trevor would follow. He was silent for a few seconds, debating the liabilities of discussing Hannah with Trevor. Finally he said, "This one is different, Trev. All I can think about is being with her."

Trevor sighed deeply. No fun with Colt today, he thought, watching a glaze of lovesickness spread across his brother's face. He shook his head. He considered himself pretty worldly for a Virginia country boy, but it wouldn't take someone who knew women as well as he did to recognize that Colt was in love—and in way over his head.

"You want me to shoot you now, or wait until after she breaks your heart?" he asked, knowing from experience that it was better to be a love-'em-and-leave-'em type of fella.

"She's not like that. She's different."

"Right. And she doesn't know that you own half the car dealerships in Richmond and Roanoke or that you build million-dollar race cars or that you sit on the boards of trustees of three banks and a private school, either, does she?"

Colt scowled and thought aloud. "No, she probably doesn't."

"What. You think being rich might be a problem for her?"

"Hell, I don't know if it will or not. I hadn't really thought about it."

"You should," Trevor said, cautioning him. "You should also go slow. This is a new track for you, brother. Take it easy till you get a feel for it."

He shook his head. "I know this track. I've driven it a thousand times in my mind, and it's a sure win."

"So was Martinsville."

Colt's eyes were suddenly cold and hard with memories, but he didn't speak. He didn't have to. Both brothers knew the pain that came with being bold, brash, and brazen.

"You're nuts," Willie said, nudging the lower half of Hannah's body with her foot. "You know that, don't you?"

Hannah had the upper half of her body under the car, so Willie knew she hadn't been heard. But it didn't really matter. Willie had a tendency to speak her mind whether anyone was listening to her or not.

"One more minute," Hannah said distractedly. "There's a little metal rod here that's not in the book. It's close to this crankshaft thing. Do you suppose they're connected?"

"Well, how should I know," Willie said, even though she hadn't been expected to answer. But it was like that sometimes with Hannah liking to talk almost as much as Willie did. "Better yet, ask me if I care."

"Shoot," Hannah said, wiggling out from under the car. "I'll have to wait until Daddy comes over, and ask him." She laughed. "He's going to love that. I'll finally be the son he always wanted."

She got to her feet and smeared black goo across one cheek as she pushed her hair away from her face. Then she rubbed her chin with the back of her hand and left a light smudge of grease there.

"I wish I had more time," she said while Willie stood and calmly watched her blacken her face. "I'll never learn all there is to know about cars before Tuesday. He'll think I'm stupid."

Willie screwed up her face in disagreement. "He'll think you're a woman," she said. By habit, she also cued her speech for sounds or words that were difficult to lip-read. "It makes men nervous when women know too much about cars. It's like cars are supposed to be these mysterious machines that only men know about, so they can get together and talk about pistons and cams and rear ends, and then if there are any women around, they can think they're talking in code or something."

Hannah chuckled. "Well, I won't be making anyone nervous. I can't make heads or tails of this manual." She glanced down at the book in her hand and back at Willie, grinning. "A man wrote it."

"Break the code, and it'll probably read like a cookbook." Willie scowled and gazed across the driveway to the street beyond. "Speaking of kooks, I wonder what's keeping my mother. She should have been home long ago."

The relationship between Willie and her mother was a queer one in Hannah's opinion. From the time Hannah had first met the pair nine years earlier, it struck her that Willie seemed to have assumed the adult role. Wondering where her mother was was nothing new. As a twelve-year-old she had sat on Hannah's back porch and wondered the same thing countless times, never really worrying, merely wondering.

Left to her own devices much of the time, Willie had become accustomed to having, doing, and thinking about things her own way. And one of the things she was emphatic about was that she wasn't anything like her mother. Willie described her mother as being a flake, an airhead . . . and various other labels that basically meant she wasn't a stable person. And for the most part Hannah had to agree. But then again, Willie wasn't exactly anchored in bedrock either.

But as with oil and vinegar, which possess many of the same characteristics—clear and liquid, great on salads—but don't mix well unless you shake them, such was the relationship between Willie and her mother. Together they fought constantly about everything from political issues to who last took out the garbage. While the mother was extremely liberal in her thinking and called herself a political activist, the daughter took a staunch conservative stand on most topics and called herself a member of the silent majority. But they were always there for each other, Hannah had noticed over the years. Willie's mother provided a home, clothes, and food for her daughter, and Willie never failed to bail her mother out of jail when she was arrested during this or that protest.

"What is your mother saving this week?" Hannah asked.

"A pet cemetery."

"What?"

"The state wants to build a road over this old pet cemetery, so this vet and my mother and maybe a dozen other people are going to chain themselves to this monument that was erected for a dog named Gus and wait—" She looked over Hannah's shoulder at a car pulling into the driveway. Hannah turned too. "Ah. Lookee here who's come to call," Willie said.

A sporty white Trans Am slowed to a stop not two yards from where Hannah stood feeling thrilled, nervous, and incredibly dirty.

Colt got out. He was smiling broadly at first, but as his gaze took in the fact that Hannah looked a little like one of his mechanics, he frowned.

"What's this?" he asked. "Having car trouble?"

Hannah watched him walk toward her and got a sharp impression that there was something different about him. He waved and said something to Willie. And when Hannah didn't speak, but stood staring at him in deep concentration, he smiled. "Surprised to see me?"

She saw every word he said.

As if struck by lightning, she gasped out, "Your moustache. You shaved."

"What do you think?" he asked, self-conscious, unsure of how she'd react to the change in his appearance and completely unaware of\how much more handsome he was without the moustache.

"I think I like it." She did like it. What she liked more, however, was the fact that he'd clearly shaved the hair off his lip for her.

"Watch this," he said. With hands in front of his chest, fingertips facing outward, he inverted his hands upward, saying, "How," then he crossed two fingers, putting them to his lips and moving them directly outward, saying, "are," then he pointed to her. "You," he said, and then grinned proudly.

She lowered her eyes and bit her lower lip, genuinely pleased by his efforts, and deeply moved. She looked back at him, and using both her hands and her voice said, "That's very good."

"I know that one too," he said, indicating the sign for good. "The one I haven't learned yet is, 'you're a mess.'"

"A what?"

"You're filthy." His expression told her how much so.

With a shaky little laugh she smeared more grease on her cheek.

"What have you been doing?" he asked, taking her hand in his, turning the palm up so she could see what she'd been applying to her face.

Dismayed, she looked around for something to clean her hands with. "I've been learning about cars."

"Why?" he asked her back.

"So you won't think she's stupid," Willie answered for her.

He nodded his understanding with an amused smirk on his newly uncovered lips as Hannah continued to speak.

"I need to know what I'm taking pictures of, and I'm afraid I don't know that much about engines and car racing," she said, finding nothing to wipe her hands on and holding them away from her in disgust.

"That's okay. You help me learn to sign, and I'll teach you more than you'll ever want to know about cars and racing."

"Deal," she said, purposefully holding her hand

out to shake on the bargain. He moved to take it, then jerked back and shook his finger at her as if she were a naughty little girl.

They laughed. With grimy hand movements and clean-shaven facial responses they agreed to go inside.

"Ah. Excuse me," Willie said, feeling like a third wheel but wanting to be helpful. "Can you two, ah, handle this by yourselves? Or do you want me to hang around?"

In silent, mutual agreement they decided that whatever was about to transpire between them would come about much easier without a third party.

"Thanks, Willie," Hannah said, shaking her head but smiling her gratitude, not oblivious to the knowledge that she was as happy as Willie wanted to be. "You're a good friend."

"Hannah?" Willie said. "I almost forgot to tell you. . . . Peter called again. He wants to know what to tell Sheila Merritt."

Hannah's spirits plummeted. Why wouldn't they leave her alone? she asked herself, recognizing the tightness in her chest. Showing her pictures to Sheila Merritt was the opportunity she'd been working so hard for. She knew if she let it pass that it might not ever come again. She knew, but . . .

"Tell him I haven't decided yet."

Hannah's house was located in the middle of the first block off one of Richmond's busiest commercial thoroughfares. It hadn't been hard for Colt to locate, not with the tasteful sign in the front yard that read "Photography by Alexander."

Other than the fact that her home also housed her business, it looked very much like anyone else's. He hadn't really thought about all the devices a deaf person might need to live alone, but the ordinariness of Hannah's home brought it forcefully to mind.

He knew that the lights were wired to flash when the doorbell or telephone rang, and that she had a Telecommunications Device for the Deaf that was more like a typewriter than a telephone, and he suspected there were other gadgets and contraptions built in or discreetly set around to help her. But while Hannah scrubbed industriously to get the grease off her hands, Colt was once again struck with a sense of regret and inadequacy in all the things he didn't know about her and the world she lived in.

"Would you like some coffee?" she asked from the kitchen doorway, watching him as he moved from photo to photo in her studio, studying her work from the collection on her walls.

He turned to face her and dramatically signed, "Yes. Thank you." *Good* and *thank you* were his best signs, because they were easy to remember, being very much alike.

"You'll be a pro in no time," she said.

"Well, I figured that sign would come in handy," he said. She'd been bound to offer him *something* eventually, but to tell the truth, in his fantasies he'd been leaning toward, *Would you like to kiss me?* "Yes, thank you." And, *Is now a good time for you to ravish my body?* "Yes, thank you."

"Who's Peter?" he blurted out. It was something he hadn't wanted to ask but was dying to know.

"My agent."

"Oh." He also wanted to ask if their relationship was purely business, but he was on a straightaway now, and didn't want to push his luck in the curves too soon.

She smiled at him before she went back into the kitchen. He followed her, detaining her as she filled a pot with water.

"Sign to me when you speak, okay? The book I bought says I need to see it and use it as much as possible, or I'll forget."

"That's true," she said, signing, aware that the lessons had begun, and that he would have many questions. Colt wasn't the first hearing person she'd met who had no knowledge of deafness other than as some abstract concept labeled "handicap." "When I don't talk to my deaf friends for a while, I get rusty at it. And they're much better at it than I am, because I don't always use it."

She went back to making coffee, and Colt leaned back against the sink to watch her. He wondered if he'd ever tire of looking at her. There was a grace in her movements that reminded him of a ballet. Though no expert on ballet—his tastes ran in another direction entirely—he'd always admired the fluidity and poise of the dancers. Hannah had both. And watching her, he could well appreciate what people went to the ballet to see.

"Why are you here?" Hannah asked, voicing the question that had been on the tip of her tongue since he'd arrived. "Have you changed your mind about Tuesday?"

"No. I just wanted to see you," he said, signing the last two words.

Her skin grew warm, and she experienced a loose lifting sensation in her midsection as his gaze roamed over her face, then lingered on her mouth.

To cover her sudden disquiet, she curled her outstretched fingers and drew them toward her, saying, "This is the sign for want, wants, wanted . . . don't want, too, if you frown or shake your head at the same time."

Still looking at her as if he were a starving man at a feast prepared for a king, he silently signed, "I want you."

He's a quick learner, she thought as he pushed himself upright and stepped toward her. She swallowed hard while her heart seemed to spin in her chest and beat at erratic intervals.

She stood like a tree, rooted to the floor, helpless and completely at his mercy. She had no thoughts. She felt incapable of speech or movement. Yet deep within her a life energy surged through her veins, changing who and what she was, altering the world she lived in. And he became the sun and the rain to her.

He put his hand to her cheek, and she leaned into his warmth and intensity, stretching and aching for more. His lips touched hers with the gentleness of early morning dew, and she drank thirstily. He showered her face with kisses, then returned to her mouth. His tongue penetrated her lips to feed and nourish the passion and sensuality she kept composed and idle inside of her.

He stepped away slowly, and she released a long, shuddering breath. They shared a moment of needing and wanting, regarding each other with immeasurable awe and insightfulness.

In stunned silence she watched as he unbuttoned the front of his shirt and pulled it from the waistband of his slacks. She took in the golden brown skin that covered the smooth, rippling contours of his chest. She sensed the potential for strength and force in him, but it didn't frighten her. Dark, spongy hair covered his torso and tapered low into his pants—and that didn't frighten her either.

His hands, as they moved through the air toward her, caught and held her attention. They stopped, but only for an instant, before they grasped the hem of her yellow T-shirt. She lifted her gaze to look back into his eyes, to see the emotions that were so like her own. Still, all she could execute willfully was the steady in-and-out breathing of her lungs. In and out. In and out.

He pulled her closer, and then slowly raised the bottom of her shirt up over her head. With a hand to the warm flesh of her back, he pulled the shirt free of her hair with the other. Pale, barely sun-kissed skin beckoned his touch. He released the clasp of her bra, and with both hands outlined the slender curve of her neck and the smooth slope of her shoulders, pushing the straps and the silky material away from her.

He glanced at her firm, pink-tipped breasts and then back into her eyes. In wonder he watched as her pupils dilated and her skin flushed with excitement. His heart hammered harder and harder. The air became thin. He felt his own excruciating need between his legs. For a second he thought he was going to pass out before he could kiss her again.

She laid a hand on his chest. His body clamored for her, but in his mind—no, more in his heart—he battled for restraint. He wanted to know her. Really know her. Body, mind, and soul. He wanted to take his time and learn about her. He wanted to know where to touch her and how to kiss her to give her the most enjoyment. He wanted to see the passion and pleasure in her eyes. He wanted to hear her when she moaned with delight and cried out in ecstasy. More than for his own fulfillment he was greedy to have his name on her lips, to feel her pulling him close and to know that she needed him.

He cupped her breast with his hand and stroked the rigid tip with the pad of his thumb. When she opened her mouth with a sweet gentle gasp of sensation, he moved in, using his tongue to tease her, taste her, and torment her. She stepped closer, and his arms encircled her, pressing her flesh to his. He deepened the kiss, stole her life's breath, and waited for her to ask for more.

Hannah's head reeled. A nonthreatening darkness engulfed her as she gave herself up to him. Radiant shivers passed through her body in waves, curling and cresting low in her pelvis. She was hot and aching and weak. She reached out to him, circling her arms about his neck, holding him close, wanting to be a part of him.

He bent and lifted her into his arms, burying his face in the warmth of her neck. She nibbled indiscriminately on his neck and the lobe of his ear, and she felt his laughter in his chest. She looked at him and trembled with excitement at the triumphant expression on his face.

He kissed her again when they stood at the foot of the stairs leading to the second floor and her bedroom. He fell back against the wall, taking his time, lingering in the taste of her. She started when his knees gave way and they sank slowly onto the first step.

They pressed their heads together in an intimate moment of fun and laughter. He was still smiling when he looked at her, happier and more content than he had been in years, but wanting her more than he wanted to breathe.

She watched his expression change to a tender mask of intense desire and knew what he was feeling. With her heart pounding in her throat, she disentangled her legs from his arms and stood up.

She didn't know if what they were doing was good or bad, right or wrong, wise or foolish, but she knew what her heart was yearning for, and what her body craved. She extended her hand to him, and when he took it, she turned and led him up the stairs. Without a backward glance she took him into her room and, letting his fingers slip from hers, went to stand beside the bed.

She slipped out of her shoes before she stepped

back to face him. She glanced down and with clumsy, trembling fingers loosened the snap and zipper of her jeans. His hands covered hers, and she looked up into eyes brimming with love and profound sensitivity. He lowered his mouth to hers.

With his mouth and his hands he transported her through a mystical mirage. An optical phenomenon in slow motion. A reflection of his passion that was so real, she could feel it and taste it. He generated heat with his touch and scorched her with his lips. In a timeless void, she lay naked on the bed and watched him remove his clothes as if he were an unattainable illusion. Strong, proud, and perfect. He loomed above her, real and tangible. He set her on fire. She opened herself to him, and he plunged deep within her. Hard and hot, he drove deeper and deeper into her body, piercing her mind to touch her soul. As the heat became unbearable, the mirage exploded into a puff of air that moved languorously in ascending waves, taking Hannah with it.

Colt was smokin'—and he didn't even have a cigarette. He rolled off Hannah, leaving one arm curved around her body and flinging the other across his face. He was too happy, too satisfied, too contented to actually feel anything specific.

It was a warm, lazy Saturday evening in May. Birds called good night to one another outside Hannah's bedroom window. Cars passed on the street below. The glow from a bedside lamp hollowed out a hole in the darkness, a warm cocoon, a place that belonged to them alone. Life was grand, and he was a happy man as he released a long, loud groan to that effect.

Hannah, with her head on his chest, felt the vibration and raised her head. "Did you say something?"

He peeked out from under his arm at her and

smiled. He framed her face with his hands. "I said you're beautiful."

She lowered her eyes self-consciously and shrugged. "Pretty maybe, but not beautiful. I'm no . . . heart stopper," she said, recalling the description she'd read in a magazine article.

"You stopped mine."

"Well," she said, playing with the hair on his chest. "You're an exceptional man." In more ways than one, she thought.

He shook his head. "You just can't hear all the heads turning when you walk by."

She frowned, thinking she'd misunderstood him, and then saw the laughter in his eyes. Gentle, benign teasing was a form of acceptance that she recognized, and it warmed and gladdened her heart. She lowered her head to his chest, reveling in the beat of his heart against her cheek.

Colt closed his eyes and took in the night. His mind wandered aimlessly, contemplating Hannah, his life, and life in general. A bird whistled, and his thoughts lingered on the notion that Hannah hadn't heard it. It took away some of his own enjoyment. He gave her shoulders a compassionate squeeze.

She raised her head again to look at him.

"What is it like? To be deaf?" he asked.

"Very quiet," she said. It was her standard answer, meant to be flip and final. But seeing the appeal and the willingness to understand in his expression, she went on. "It's nothing," she said. "It's not a roar in my ears that gives me headaches or makes me crazy. It's more an annoyance than anything else." She stacked her hands on his chest, set her chin on top, and continued to speak. "If the whole world were deaf, it wouldn't be a problem at all. The worst of it is not being able to hear and communicate with other people."

"Were you born deaf?"

"No." She seemed to be looking back in time. "Measles. I had measles when I was six. I got very sick with a fever. I wore a hearing aid for a couple of years after that, but then I couldn't hear even very loud sounds."

"Did you go to schools for the deaf then?" he asked, trying to get a picture of what it was like for her growing up.

She shook her head. It was nice to feel his arms around her and to talk, knowing that he was listening.

"My mother went to a lot of trouble to make sure that everything went on as it had before I got sick," she said, her memory drifting back twenty years.

Being mainstreamed through the public school system had been very painful at times, though she'd never told her mother. It had long since ceased to be something she couldn't talk about. She'd been set apart and different from the other children. And children could be cruel. To please her parents, and because she had no other options, she learned to lip-read as best she could. In keeping with her mother's concept of normalcy, speech therapy was like an extracurricular activity after school three times a week—on Saturday mornings she took ballet.

Eventually she could speak well enough to have friends who would listen to her, but as skilled as she became at lipreading, it was still impossible for her to read more than one set of lips at a time. Social gatherings of more than two people were nightmares for her. She couldn't always catch up with who was speaking in order to follow group conversations, catch jokes, or know when someone *wasn't* speaking, so she could add to the discussion herself. And adolescents could be cruel too.

She grew up alone, introverted, and always feeling awkward. Still, there were pockets of happiness. He father provided many of them. He hadn't felt the guilt over Hannah's loss the way her mother had. And although he had complied with his wife's wishes to force their daughter into the established norm, it had been very different when the two of them were alone. She hadn't always had to read his lips when he spoke. He would sometimes write down his advice to her or the long, complicated theories he had about things. He hadn't constantly corrected her or insisted that she do things a certain way to cover up her deafness. And always, always, there had been the affectionate wink from him when her mother was upset about something that Hannah had done or not done.

Her maternal grandmother, too, had been an understanding soul. And ultimately, she'd been the person to open the new doors in Hannah's silent world.

"So your grandmother gave you your first camera," Colt repeated, listening carefully to her story, knowing that she'd left volumes of her past between the lines. "I was going to ask how you got into photography."

"It was a very special day for me," she said. "My parents had to go out of town on business. My father was looking for a new job because he'd just been laid off from his other one. We were going to have to move, and it wasn't the greatest of times." She recalled the fears she'd had of facing new people, attending a new school, and having to build her world all over again.

"Anyway," she continued, "my parents left me with my grandmother, and it was my birthday. We had a party." She smiled. "She gave me my camera, and she invited a deaf woman over to her house to meet me."

"You'd never met any other deaf people?"

"No. There were two other deaf children at my

school, but they were older, and like me they kept to themselves. They wouldn't have heard what I was saying, even if I'd talked to them."

"Why not?" he asked, without thinking.

She grinned at him. "They were deaf too."

He frowned.

"I know. It's crazy, isn't it? This lady and I sat at my grandmother's kitchen table and just stared at each other for a long time. Here we were, two deaf people, and we couldn't communicate with each other."

"So what happened?"

Hannah chuckled. "She looked straight at me and started waving her hands around. I thought she was nuts."

"Sign language," he guessed. "How old were you?"

She nodded. "Fifteen. That was when I really started my education. We moved down here shortly after that, and one of the first places I learned to get to was the library. I found a book on sign language and a book full of resources and contacts for deaf people. I'd always thought that there was just me and a couple of other people who couldn't hear. Imagine how surprised I was to find out that there are millions of us, and that there are special schools and even a university for us."

"Your parents hadn't told you?"

"No. I never asked. And they must have thought that it wasn't important. And my mother . . ." her voice trailed away.

"What about her?"

"My mother wouldn't have let me go anyway," she said, and then she quickly amended her statement. "Not that she didn't love me. She did. She lived for me. She taught me how to eat quietly and set pots and pans down quietly. How to laugh so it wasn't too loud. How to keep my voice low. How to walk. How to be . . . alert all the time. A million things she taught me, so no one could tell I was deaf."

"So no one could hurt you," he guessed again from the tender expression on her face.

"She meant well," she said. "But she couldn't teach me how to *be* deaf." She sat up, pulling the covers around her. "Shew! After I found out about the other deaf people, all we did was fight. For years." She grinned. "We ganged up on her. Me and my father and my grandmother. I went to a deaf high school my last two years, and my father arranged to get funding so that I could go to Gallaudet." She shook her head. "That's when the fighting really got bad. Are you hungry?"

Taken off guard, he nodded, and watched her put on a short floral print wrap that he never wanted to forget seeing her in.

"What happened? What's Gallaudet? Why did it get worse?" he asked, pulling on only his slacks and following her down the stairs. He had to reask the questions on the bottom step.

"Boy!" she said, only half teasing. "You really don't know anything, do you?" He knew what she meant and couldn't argue. She knew he couldn't and continued to speak as they moved into the kitchen. "Gallaudet just happens to be a very famous deaf university. It's in Washington D.C. It has mostly deaf students, and it's geared totally to the service of the hearing impaired. Only a few of the teachers are deaf, but someday it'll have mostly deaf teachers too. And . . ."

"Okay. Okay. I get the picture." He took the apple she offered him. "So what was the problem?"

"My mother couldn't let go. Would you rather have a sandwich? I want more than just this apple," she said, leaning into the refrigerator. Colt took a deep breath as he watched the hem of her robe ride up. "Just about the time I graduated she was finally getting used to the idea that I was with other deaf people and in a semiprotected environment. But that was after a zillion trips back and forth between here and D.C. and almost as many phone calls to my advisers at school. Even when I decided to study photography and transferred to NTID in Rochester—that's the National Technical Institute for the Deaf—" she told him pointedly, "she was constantly checking up on me. And in all that time she never once considered that I might do anything but move back home when I was finished."

"Uh-oh," he muttered, using Willie's phraseology as he guessed at what came next. He pointed to mayonnaise and mustard for his ham sandwich, and she went on.

"I'd thought about going to New York and becoming famous," she said with a grin. "But my mother would have gone insane. Even moving here and setting up the kind of life I wanted wasn't as easy as I'd hoped it would be."

"Why not?"

"I'm deaf, but I wanted to succeed in the hearing world. It's easier to survive if you stay in the deaf world. Deaf people understand deaf people. They help each other and support one another and keep mostly to themselves. It's very frustrating trying to get along in the hearing world when no one can or wants to take the time to understand you."

Colt tried to remember if he'd ever turned away from someone whose speech he couldn't understand, or if he'd ever failed to help someone who obviously needed help understanding what was being said to them. He couldn't recall a specific instance, but he was willing to admit that he might have out of sheer ignorance.

"Will you look at that," she said in disgust. She was looking out the kitchen window at her car.

He leaned over her shoulder, glanced at the car, and then back at her. "What?"

"Well, it's sitting there like of lump of junk, reminding me that I should be out there going over its pistons and distributors with a flashlight, instead of in here playing with you."

"It only has one distributor, Hannah. And which would you rather be doing? Getting filthy dirty out there with it or getting filthy dirty in here with me?" he asked, sliding a hand up under her robe.

Yes indeed, it was one warm, lazy Saturday night in May they spent together. They talked a little more and loved a little more. And little more by little more, they came to know each other.

She asked how he'd gotten into car racing, and he told her about his father and growing up in the Virginia countryside. He recalled for her his life on a struggling farm where they grew corn and apples and spent weekends eating dust at dirt tracks all over the southeast. He remembered for her images of his father, knee-deep into auto parts, bent over an engine or euphoric at the tracks—and then admitted that he and his brother had spent much of their youth the same way.

However, where his father had raced merely for the joy of it, Colt's joy came from the competition. He raced to win. And the dirt tracks hadn't held his interest for long. He'd been on the Sportsman circuit by the time he was eighteen, driving cars that he'd worked on but that belonged to someone else.

His big break had come when he'd hooked up with a crusty pair of garage mechanics who'd known a man by the name of Joe Mallini. Joe eventually had owned three modified road cars. He'd driven one himself, Colt had driven the second, and later he'd taken Trevor on to drive the third.

For six years the three of them had been regulars on tracks all over the country, with Colt consistently taking one of the top three spots and bringing home the big bucks. The friendship between the three of them had been thick and strong. The names Mallini and McKinnon had become interchangeable, both off and on the track. They'd become partners in everything—except with the ladies, of course. Then it had been each man for himself.

"Does racing ever scare you?" Hannah asked, sitting cross-legged on the bed across from Colt, watching him as he spoke. The black of night had settled in. With little difficulty they'd filled the hours with words.

The few phrases Hannah hadn't understood, Colt had matter-of-factly illustrated with gestures or written on paper as if being misconstrued was something common in his life. She knew differently, which made his attitude all the more pivotal in her ever-growing capability to trust him.

"I don't race anymore," he said, throwing his legs off the bed and walking to the window to peer out at the darkness.

"Why not?" she asked, taking notice of an unexpected tension in his shoulders.

He shrugged, turning to her to speak. "The business end of it got to be too big. Someone had to take over and handle it full time. And Trevor's an idiot."

"Your brother?"

He grinned. "He's not really an idiot." He sat down on the bed beside her. "He's just not interested in the business. He'd rather race cars and chase girls—and in that order."

"And he's a good driver?"

"We're having the best year we've ever had. He's still young, and he gets better every year."

"Do you miss it?"

He shook his head, and Hannah's eyes narrowed in concern. He'd broken eye contact with her, as if his answer wasn't entirely the truth.

"Actually, I've been getting as big a thrill out of owning the cars, getting better and faster cars built, and gathering up a top-notch crew," he said with some real enthusiasm. "Putting together a winning team can be just as tricky and just as rewarding as driving."

"Tell me about your business."

He hyperextended his neck to look at the ceiling as if wondering what he should tell her, or where to start.

"We own a couple of car dealerships and fast-food franchises. Flynn's at the beach, a couple of other things. Mostly my job involves running around making sure that everyone else is doing their job and making us money."

"So you . . . you're well-off?"

He smiled into her eyes, knowing she wasn't a gold digger and knowing that he wouldn't have cared if she were.

"There's always plenty of meat on the table, and I usually have lots left over for dessert, if that's what you mean," he said. He hesitated briefly as his fingers inched their way across the bedspread to dally with the ends of her sash. "As a rule I'm pretty careful about desserts though. I'm health conscious, and too many sweets can be deadly, you know. Lately though . . ."—he looked shamefaced—". . . lately I just can't seem to get enough of them."

Hannah gnawed on the insides of her cheeks to keep from smiling as she recognized the glimmer in his eyes.

"Willpower. That's what you need," she said, slowly running her finger down the front of his chest.

He sucked in a deep breath, and she smiled artfully.

"Willpower," he said, taking the word under advisement while he pulled the loose knot at her waist free. His eyes lowered to the gap he'd made in her robe. He measured the distance from her navel to her sternum with his thumb before he cradled her left breast in the palm of his hand and guided her gently back onto the sheets once more.

"I'll show you willpower," he said as his mouth closed over hers.

Five

"Don't you have to go to work or something today?" Hannah asked, squealing when Colt's arm snaked around her waist and he pulled her backward onto the bed again. It was Monday morning, and they were both a little amazed at how quickly the past forty hours had gone by, not to mention the fact that they'd spent those forty hours sequestered together from the rest of the world.

"I have something to do today, but it isn't what I'd call work," he said, leaning over her on one arm, trying to remember the last time he'd spent nearly two whole days in bed with a beautiful woman—and wondering when Hannah would let him do it with her again. "Besides, I'm the boss. I don't have to keep regular hours."

"Well, la-de-da. I'm a boss too," she said, giggling as he retaliated with a gripping pressure at her ribs. "I do keep regular hours, and if we're not careful, Willie's going to come over and catch us still in bed."

"My car's in the driveway. She'll see it and wait for me to leave."

"You think so?" she asked, knowing better.

"Sure. She's got weird hair, but she knows when she's not wanted," he said, thinking of the girl's discretion on Saturday and mentally thanking her for it. He'd never felt as young and alive as he did at that moment.

"She doesn't have weird hair," Hannah protested. Her hips shifted involuntarily at the feel of his hand meandering up her inner thigh. "Lots of women spend hours in beauty shops trying to get hair as curly as hers—they'd kill to have it naturally."

"You have lots of curly hair," he said, pulling several dark auburn strands of it through his fingers. "And you don't look like a frizzy bushwoman."

"Mine's not . . . natural." She was getting breathless. "If I get frizzed, I can get . . . my money back."

"Mm." He took a lengthy lick of the sweet warm flesh between her breasts before looking at her to speak. "There's nothing else about you that's not natural. I've checked."

"It's . . . ah . . . amazing what they can do with a glass eye these days . . . isn't it?"

He looked long and hard into the depths of her eyes, well aware that no mere mortal could create anything as clear and sagacious. They were his link to the thoughts she was willing to share with him, to the joy in her soul, and to the passion in her heart. They were what first attracted him to her, one of the things he loved best about her.

Without breaking eye contact, he covered her body with his, stretching her arms well above her head. He nuzzled her cheek and began to work his lips along the smooth curve of her jaw to her neck.

"Hey," Willie's voice sounded from the floor below. "Hope y'all are decent up there, cuz I'm on my way up."

The look on Colt's face was indescribable. He

quickly pulled the front of her wrap together and rolled away. Propping on one arm above a giggling Hannah, he appeared unsullied and un-ruffled when Willie peeked around the corner.

"Thank goodness," she said on a huge burst of breath as her hand covered her heart and she went limp on the doorjamb. "I wasn't sure if I wanted to come up here or not," she admitted, looking sincerely ill at ease. She glanced from Colt to Hannah twice before she addressed the latter. "It's eight-thirty, and we have that ten o'clock at the park today."

"I know," Hannah said, still grinning at Colt's reaction. "I'll hurry."

"What's happening at the park at ten o'clock?" asked Colt.

"We're doing some photos for a back-to-school sale at a children's clothing store."

"And you don't keep kids waiting," Willie added. "They get real nasty."

"How long will it take?" he wanted to know, planning his day around hers so he could get back to her as soon as possible.

"Three or four hours," she said. "Then we'll finish the rest here."

"How long will you be in the darkroom?"

"I won't do that until later tonight."

"I thought that's what you were going to do all afternoon," he said, confused.

She shook her head. "We'll do the modeled stuff this morning. The catalog stuff this afternoon and maybe tomorrow afternoon, too, depending on how much there is. Then I'll develop what I have later, after Willie leaves."

"She hates the catalog stuff, so it takes her forever," said Willie, impatient and restless just thinking about it. "I'll start loading the car. Need anything special?"

"I don't think so. Thanks."

They both thought she'd leave then, but she stayed. After a few moments of reflective silence, her lips curled into a smirk, and she asked, "This brother of yours? Are his lessons in popular mechanics anything like yours?"

Colt purposely returned to Hannah's house around the dinner hour, knowing that Hannah would have to stop to eat eventually. And as they'd left the day and time of their next meeting open and dependent on their schedules, he came armed with an excuse to see her.

"Well I was just thinking that even though you don't need to know how a car actually runs, you should probably know a little about racing before we go to Roanoke on Thursday. So you'll know what's important to get pictures of and what's not," he said, thinking his grounds for being there sounded flimsy and trumped up when they were stated aloud, certainly not as crucial as they'd sounded several hours earlier when they'd popped into his head. "And . . . well, I thought that maybe when you stopped for dinner, I could explain it to you. You haven't eaten yet, have you?"

Willies tucked her tongue in her cheek and turned, pretending to rearrange the child-sized cardigans and turtleneck shirts on one of the two tables they'd set up in the studio. Lights were situated around the other, and Hannah, as she stood perched on a ladder with a camera in her hand, bent over the table to get her shot. She, however, wasn't pretending anything.

"I am so glad to see you," she said miserably. "I was hoping you'd come back and take me away from all this."

That was all Colt needed. "Great," he said, his easy grin showing off his dimples. "Come on down from there, and I'll take you out to dinner."

She did, putting her camera on the table and turning off the bright lights as she went, talking all the while.

"I really, really hate this stuff," she said, her strong feelings making her careless about her speech and causing her to put hard *w*'s where there should have been *r*'s in her words. "Over and over and over, the same old stuff. And all it does is lie there."

"This is how catalog pictures are taken, huh?" He walked over to inspect the tables.

"Once in a while, it might not be so bad," she continued, not having seen him speak. "But all the time . . ." She finished her sentence with a frustrated noise and exaggerated arm movements.

"If you don't like it, why do it? There are other things you can do with a camera, aren't there? School pictures. Couldn't you work strictly with models or something? Or do portraits? Those in the other room are great," Colt said.

The two women exchanged a brief unreadable glance before Hannah answered him, her agitation no longer evident.

"I do this because I like to eat, and because someone needs to pay the mortgage on the house. And I'd do more of it if I could, because I don't pay my loyal assistant enough as it is."

"It's enough," Willie said without looking up. Colt glanced at her with a clear view for the first time.

"Did she tell you that I pay her enough?" Hannah asked, catching his eye movement. He nodded. "You have to watch her. She fibs—a lot."

Willie simply shook her head.

Hannah looked almost angry when she continued to speak. Even her words were a bit harsh. "If she couldn't drive my car whenever she needed one, and if she couldn't live next door with her mother, she'd have to get some other job. But she stays with me—because she loves me."

Willie looked up wearily, as if she'd gone into the same battle a hundred time before.

"The one you really ought to watch is her," Willie told Colt, shaking an accusing finger at Hannah. "She nags."

"Ha!"

"You do," she insisted. "My mother doesn't nag me as much as you do."

"Ha!"

"You know what I want. You know I like doing what I'm doing with you. I don't want to go to college and get some huge career job that'll suck the life out of me before I'm thirty. I want to stay here, and I want to keep working with you. I'm happy here." She paused and grinned. "Besides, if I try to go somewhere else, I'll have to fill out an application for work."

"Oh!" Hannah threw her hands up in exasperation and defeat.

"What?" Colt asked, intrigued by the discussion.

"Oh," she said again much in the same manner. "She hates filling out forms that need her legal name on them."

He looked at Willie, his eyes twinkling with laughter and new interest. She had weird hair, and she was a little strange in manner for his tastes, but he was forming a deep liking for her. He was beginning to suspect that her real name was just as odd as she was, but he didn't care if it was Rumpelstiltskin. He had a feeling that both women were valid in their arguments. Willie was happy with Hannah, and she stayed because she loved her.

"You ought to try growing up with 'Colton,'" he said, backing Willie because he believed in her true motives, and because he liked the idea of Hannah having such a good friend around. "It got my nose broken for me twice."

"Really?" she said. "Colton's not so bad. If you'd gotten stuck with my name, you'd probably be dead by now."

He staged a look of horror for her. "It's that bad?"

"It's that bad." Her face was solemn and pitiful.

"It's a cute name," Hannah said, grinning playfully. "Tell him what it is, Willie."

"Not in your lifetime." She was vehement. "Why don't you two go eat and stop picking on me. My mother's been out politically activating the government again today, and losing two hopeless battles in a row always ticks her off. I'm going to need my energy."

"Losing the pet cemetery doesn't mean she's going to lose that little apple orchard," Hannah said. "People like trees. Maybe more will show up to help this time."

There was a brief discourse in which Colt was filled in on Willie's mother's devout belief in an American's right to protest, and a few of her other favorite personal and political creeds. He was quick to get the picture of Willie's unorthodox background.

"Why don't you come with us," Colt suggested. "I'll need your help explaining racing and NASCAR to Hannah." When she looked about to decline, he pleaded. "Please. It's either you or a pad and pencil, because I haven't learned enough sign language yet. And you need to eat anyway."

"Come," Hannah chimed in. She didn't have to force her encouraging smile, but she was aware of a particular lack of enthusiasm to have Willie with them.

She hadn't lied when she'd said she was glad to see him. He'd occupied her every thought during the day. Over and over she'd relived their moments together, every touch, every word, recalling the night they'd met and remembering how familiar he'd seemed to her.

It hadn't been his face that she'd recognized, she'd come to realize. It was *him*. His character. The kindness and tolerance in him. His dignity, courage, and fortitude. She'd trusted him instantly because somehow she'd identified his goodness and compassion. She'd put her hand in his and allowed him to lead her because she'd felt his strength and control. She'd seen him a million times in her dreams, this man. Not his face, but who and what he was inside.

Her heart had recognized him the night they'd first met. It had taken him in and loved him immediately, cherished his presence, rejoiced in his coming at last. But unlike his heart, hers was greedy and selfish. She didn't want to share him with anyone. She wanted his undivided attention. She wanted to possess him completely.

Reason and logic told her that Willie was no threat. She knew Willie, and she loved her. It told her, too, that love was fragile and easily crushed. A dark side of her warred with all she knew and believed to be true of the emotions she felt for Colt. Jealousy left a sharp taste in her mouth.

In the end the three of them went to a quiet neighborhood restaurant. It was a simple place, with simple food and plenty of friendly, simple conversation.

Simple conversation? For Hannah and Willie, understanding NASCAR racing from a male point of view was like . . . well, it was like trying to understand a car engine!

There were points in Colt's cram-course that were as obvious as windshield wipers and tires. The object of the race was to beat the other cars around the track. The best driver with the fastest car usually did that, but it was also an extremely dangerous sport in which a multitude of complications and calamities could occur. So no man was an automatic winner.

It made sense to them when he explained about the sponsors who financed both the drivers and specific races to keep the sport going.

After that he gave them a few facts about the sport that they'd actually heard before, but like batteries, filters, and spark plugs, they'd rarely given any thought to. There were different types of tracks—dirt and hard surface—although all the official NASCAR races were on hard surfaces. Some tracks were bigger than others, and part of the race's . . . charm, so to speak, was the endurance levels of both the driver and the car. In the NASCAR series races they traveled anywhere from 150 miles to 500 miles on tracks ranging in size from one-half mile to two and a half miles around.

When he explained that in order to drive five hundred miles on a two-and-a-half-mile track, the driver had to go around the track two *hundred* times and use up as many as twelve to sixteen or more tires and lord knew how many gallons of gas and oil, the two women sent covert glances to each other. With female telepathy they agreed that one quick spin around the track would save a lot of time, energy, and natural resources, and accomplish much the same thing.

They were glad to hear that in order to win a series title, as in the Winston Cup or the Busch Grand National, the cars and drivers didn't have to participate in every race on the schedule, nor did they have to win every race. Winning was determined by an overall point system dependent primarily on the number of races entered and the finish position of each entry. They were convinced that someone's wife or mother had been instrumental in the instigation of such an equitable long-term contest.

Then it was back to the cams-and-pistons code

as he launched into their education on the impor-
tance of the aerodynamic contours of the car,
cubic inches of motor, manifolds, fuel-injection
pumps, nitrous oxide, and compression. Hannah
tried to make sense of it, truly she did. But either
Willie wasn't making heads or tails of it any better
than she was, or the things Colt was describing
to them were incomprehensible in at least two
languages—English and sign. Maybe if she knew
Greek . . .

"Oh, pa-leeeese," Willie finally said with a groan,
rubbing her arms and holding them close. "Stop
already. My arms are so worn out, they're throb-
bing."

"Sorry," he said, looking sheepish. "I've been
running my mouth too much."

"That's okay," she said. "It's a lot to absorb in one
sitting. Maybe we can finish it another time."
She winked at Hannah. She hadn't lied about the
ache in her arms, but she wasn't going to sit
through another NASCAR dissertation if she could
help it.

Talk turned to proper attire at the race tracks
while Colt paid the bill and escorted the ladies out
to his car. They bid Willie good night in the
driveway, and then kicked the gravel around with
the toes of their shoes, putting off their own
farewells.

Using only the bright light from Hannah's back
porch, they teased and laughed and enjoyed the
cooling breeze of the warm spring night. Eventually they worked their way over to the steps that led
to the back porch and sat down.

"You know, none of what I was telling you before
has anything to do with racing, really," he said
introspectively.

"Wait a minute," she said, standing to retrieve a
lawn chair from the porch, unfolding it and set-

ting it opposite the steps. "Sit here in the light so I can see you, please."

"Sorry. I wasn't thinking."

She smiled. "It's not so easy being around a deaf person, is it?"

"I'll get used to it." He was grinning with that you're-so-beautiful look on his face again. It was a signal to his thoughts and gave Hannah a rush of nervous excitement and flutters in her abdomen.

"Tell me what you were going to say," she prompted him.

He readjusted his position to lean his elbows on his knees. "I was just saying that it's the race itself that really excites everyone." A glowing light of enthusiasm shone in his eyes as he spoke. "The souped-up engines, the modifications in the cars, all the fancy rules and regulations, all the high-tech stuff . . . that all came after the race. The old guys used to drive the family cars, pickups, anything roadworthy. Back then they won just to be best in their county or best in two counties. Simply for the win. No money. Just to be able to say that they had the best car on the road, and that they were the best driver.

"It's still basically the same," he continued nostalgically. "It's all big money now. Better cars. Bigger engines. Safer too. But it doesn't really change anything. It's still the speed and outthinking the guy ahead of you. Pushing your car and your determination and courage to the limits. Going one step further than you ever dreamed you could go. . . ." His voice trailed off in remembrance.

"Giving your heart wings," Hannah said softly, more to herself than to Colt, as she identified the feelings he was talking about.

"What?" he asked.

"That . . . what you said? That's called 'giving your heart wings.' It's what Buzz Elliot feels when he climbs his mountains. It's what I feel with my cameras." She shrugged. "It's what anybody feels when they're doing what they want to be doing . . . what they *deep in their heart* want to be doing, even though they're afraid, and even when they might not succeed. My grandmother told me about it."

"She did, huh?" he said, rolling her words around in his mind and liking the sound of them. His intense gaze was encouragement for her to explain them to him.

"I want you to meet my grandmother someday," she said, her voice on the verge of laughter. "She's . . . feisty. You'd like her."

"You must be a lot like her."

"I try hard to be," she said. She stood abruptly and put her hands on Colt's shoulders. "She's one of those people who speaks very clearly, you know?" She gave him a little shake. "She took me like this. She made an awful face at me and said, 'Hannah, you're only deaf. You're young and smart and healthy and strong. You could fly if you really wanted to.'" She gave him another shake. "She said, 'You have to give your heart wings. You have to fight for what you really want, because no one can do it for you. Don't let anyone hold you down when your heart tells you it's time to be free. Don't hide what's in your heart, not for anyone.' She said, 'If you don't give your heart wings, you'll never fly.'"

Her words, with the prolonged vowels and the occasional exaggerated consonants, rang in his mind. He felt them like a thousand well-defined swords cutting into his heart. His heart, with its guilt and pain. His heart, with its secrets and fears. His heart, with its clipped and impotent wings. In his soul, where he could still recall what it was to fly free and unfettered, he knew the truth of her words.

He reached out and drew her onto his lap, hiding his face in her hair, unwilling to let her see his torment, his failure. For many long moments he simply held her, enjoying the feel of her in his arms, taking comfort in her presence.

He wanted to borrow some of her strength but couldn't bring himself to ask her for it. What if he told her what had happened—how it had happened—and she pitied him? What if he disappointed her? He wanted to tell her; he wanted to share it with someone who could understand what it was to be human, to fail, to be a coward—but Hannah's heart had wings. She was a fighter. She had courage. Now that he'd found her, he simply couldn't risk losing her. He just couldn't tell her. . . .

He sat back and pushed a swag of her dark curls away from her face.

"Was that when the three of you ganged up on your mother? You, your daddy, and your grandmother?" he asked, tucking his pain back into the chest that contained all his sorrows and fastening the lid securely.

She toyed with the small hairs at the nape of his neck. "When my grandmother stepped in to back me, she refused to discuss it anymore. My father finally made the decision to let me go to the deaf school, and . . . well, I think that broke her heart." She went silent, searching for words. "He'd always supported her before. It hurt when he opposed her. And . . . they weren't the same anymore, you know? I mean, she eventually accepted the idea, and they didn't fight anymore, but things were different between them." She bent her head. "And that was my fault," she muttered sadly.

He shook his head until she looked at him. "It would have happened anyway. What happens between two people is never the fault of a third person. Especially a child." Her sweet, full lips were too close not to kiss, so he did. "You'd have had to try and make a break for it eventually anyway, Hannah. You were born to fly."

She smiled, glad that he had that impression of her. She was doing all right. She was off the ground, but she still had miles to go before she could soar the way she did in her fantasies. Soon enough, she knew, he would discover that he was overestimating her. But in the meantime, she was glad he had that impression of her.

"And does your heart have wings, Colt McKinnon?" she asked, tracing the rim of his ear with a touch that was as light as air before locking her fingers at the back of his neck.

"With you on my lap, my whole body feels like it's about to take off." He shifted his weight in the chair to demonstrate his meaning more pointedly.

"I'm serious," she said. "Is there something you want more than anything else in the world, that you don't have yet?"

"Yes," he said, dead sober.

"What is it?"

"You."

Six

Of all the wonders life had to offer, Trevor McKinnon loved racing and women best. Both were risky, arousing, and dangerous—but they weren't interchangeable.

"Jeez. Will you get with the program?" he shouted at his brother. "You missed the dinner with the Dunlevy Hardware people on Saturday to get back to this woman, and last night you missed the meeting with Roy Garber." He turned on Colt, leaning heavily on the desk. "You're the one who told me that business was business and women were just women."

"No I didn't," Colt muttered, knowing he was in the wrong, but knowing, too, that he'd never spoken those words. "What I said was that business has to come first, or you wouldn't be able to support your women."

"Same thing."

Not quite, Colt thought, though he wasn't going to split hairs with Trevor. He'd been remiss in his duties and responsibilities the last few days, and taking a scolding from the likes of Trevor couldn't have made that more clear. Even more disparaging was the idea that he couldn't fight back by finding fault with his brother.

Trevor raced hard, played hard, drank hard on occasion, and womanized *very* hard. Unlike his brother, who was calm, calculating, and determined, Trevor had lived by the seat of his pants since the time he'd worn diapers. He had a fire in his belly and lived every day as if it were his last.

But when Colt stopped racing, the task of pleasing sponsors and maintaining an image that the sponsors felt best represented their products had fallen to Trevor. Needless to say, it was a major crimp in his life-style. It had been hard to curb his natural instincts in order to please old men who cared more about making money than they did about racing—or even a good roll in the hay.

As the responsible older brother, businessman, and car owner, it had been up to Colt to set Trevor straight. After many discussions detailing the chain of command and who paid the bills, it had finally come to a point where Trevor had to toe the line or quit racing.

He'd toed the line. Overnight Trevor had turned himself into a sponsor's dream. Young, good-looking men who raced as if they were riding a bolt of lightning, who never had more than two beers in public, who rarely said anything bad about someone else where they could be overheard by the press, and who were extremely discreet with their active social lives—well let's face it, they were hard to find. And Trevor knew it.

"I can't believe you left me holding the bag with Garber," Trevor ranted. "Lord! That man's wife is ugly. And there I was with the two of them, tellin' 'em how great we are and how responsible you are. . . ."

"Okay. I said I was sorry," Colt said, clearly browbeaten. "What else do I have to do?"

"Get us out of that shopping mall thing on Tuesday," he said quickly.

"Tuesday?" Colt reached over the top of his desk to check his calendar, then swore loudly. "You've got to go, Trev. One of us has to, and I have other plans for Tuesday."

"I know." A sly smirk. "And I'm not going if you don't."

Colt was about to tell him what could he do with his ultimatum when something stopped him. "Why not? You love struttin' around in malls with your suit on, trying to impress young, innocent women."

"The hell I do. You know my tastes run to slightly older, more . . . worldly women. Those young ones giggle all the time. And if you must know, I've got other plans for Tuesday too." Still the sly smirk. "I'm going to the farm."

"Why?" Colt asked with an uneasy feeling in his chest.

"I want to meet her."

"Her who?"

The sly smirk and a steady gaze came first, and then he said, "Who do you think? This woman who's got your head in the clouds, that's who."

"Ah." He groaned. "Do you have to?"

Trevor staged shock and insult. "Colt. I'm your brother."

"I know." He stood and walked to the window that overlooked the car dealership below. He chewed his lower lip, trying to find the exact right words he needed to tell Trevor about Hannah. He recalled his first reaction to her deafness and thought there might be an easier way to tell him.

"She's deaf," he said brusquely, no other words seeming necessary. It was just that simple.

"Okay."

"And she's special."

"Okay."

"And . . . I love her, so I don't want you doing anything to screw things up."

"Okay!"

The trip from Richmond to Roanoke took two hours on the highway. The countryside was green and lush, the sky a deep, clear blue. It was hot again, one of those days that felt more like early August, with the sun pouring straight down by midmorning, spreading its heat into the shade of the tall oak trees and into the shiny white Trans Am as it zoomed along the highway.

If one enjoyed bright sunny days, the heat on one's skin, and the wind tugging at one's hair, it might have been a marvelous day. But if one had freckles that on the rainiest of days multiplied like rabbits, and hair that looked . . . electrified at best, one could consider it a trying day. But if one had both conditions and was also subjected to the company of an obnoxious jerk, one could consider it a damn drag of a day. Willie certainly did.

Of course, the day had started out well enough. Colt and Trevor had arranged to pick the women up early. Hannah wanted as much natural light as possible for her pictures, and Colt and Trevor had things of their own to take care of, so they were all enthusiastic for the day to get under way.

Covertly they all had the jitters. Hannah was anxious to meet Colt's mother and brother—a big step in any relationship, but particularly so if you weren't going to be able to hear a word they had to say. Colt was concerned about Hannah's reaction to Trevor and vice versa. He was also looking forward to introducing her to his mother—a big step for him in a relationship, particularly so since he'd only done it twice before, the last time being the night of his senior prom.

And then there was the tense undercurrent

Willie and Trevor lent to the circumstances. Willie, a woman who knew what she wanted from life, was atwitter with the idea of spending two days with a handsome young daredevil like Trevor McKinnon. Trevor, being Trevor, was up for anything, and as usual took everything head on.

"Hi. How are you?" Trevor asked Hannah, signing the simple words as he spoke, before he turned his million-dollar grin on her.

Colt stood in stunned disbelief while Hannah fell into instant like with young Trevor McKinnon.

There was no pity, uneasiness, or hesitation in his expression when he looked at her. And though he shared certain physical features, like his smile, with his older brother, there was a sort of wild energy about him that said he took things and people as they came, because it would be a waste of his precious time to try to change them. His acceptance of Hannah was complete and unreserved. Her hearing impairment was just part of the package to him.

"Hello," she said, smiling her spontaneous affection for him. "I'm happy to meet you. Colt talks about you often."

"Then you know what a great guy I am," he said without signing in order to test her lipreadng. When she grinned and nodded, he smirked and hung a friendly arm around her shoulders, saying, "I'm surprised. He usually lies and tells all the beautiful women he meets to stay away from me."

The teasing twinkle in his eyes was charming.

"Well, he did tell me that too," she said, smiling at Colt, who did indeed look a bit perturbed with Trevor's outrageous flirting. "But I like to form my own opinions about people."

"My kinda girl."

"No. She's my kind of girl," Colt said mildly, removing Trevor's arm from Hannah's shoulder to replace it with his own. He looped his other arm around Willie, who had been standing by and quietly studying Trevor's antics. "And so is this one, so back off, Romeo."

Challenge flashed in Trevor's eyes before he lowered his gaze to Willie and scowled.

"I've seen you. . . ." He glanced back at Hannah and then to Colt. "I remember now. She's the one from Virginia Beach, and this . . ." His gaze roved over Willie's hair. ". . . I remember your hair."

Willie's shoulder muscles became rigid under Colt's arm.

"This is Willie," Colt said, squeezing her fondly. "Why don't you show them what a big strong gentleman you can be, and load all that stuff into the car."

Trevor followed the direction of Colt's pointed finger to the two suitcases and photography equipment piled neatly near the back porch. With a quick, inscrutable glance at Willie and a careless shrug, he said, "Okay," and walked toward the porch.

"Meet my mother before you make a final judgment on my family gene pool," he said with devoted warmth in his expression and merriment in his voice as he watched his brother walk away. "We think of Trevor as the family fluke."

"I'll bet," Willie muttered, turning to watch said fluke while Colt repeated his last sentence for Hannah.

"That's an awful thing to say," Hannah said, aware that he was jesting. "I like him."

"He grows on you," he said, glad and relieved that they were hitting it off. Still in jest, but as a means of telling her how important she was to him, he added, "Just don't let him grow too close."

She sighed her contentment with him and pressed her forehead to his chest. His right arm had long since been freed when Willie slipped away, so he wrapped them both around Hannah and rocked her gently, lovingly.

Willie had been watching Trevor as he prepared to impress them all with his great rippling muscles and strength by carrying the whole load of suit-cases and equipment to the car at once. Part of her enjoyed the show very much, but the rest was pragmatic enough to see that he couldn't carry it all safely. And Hannah's cameras paid her salary.

As a rule Willie liked men. Her greatest ambition was to marry one someday. A rich one preferably, but definitely one who excited her. She tolerated their silly macho acts as something they had to do to maintain their male egos and libidos. Like their cams-and-pistons routine. But in Trevor McKin-non, she found it unreasonably irritating in the extreme.

With a much put-upon sigh, she marched over to the porch and snatched Hannah's camera bag off his shoulder, grappling with his grasp on her suitcase to get the bag away from him.

"Wait a sec," he said, setting the suitcase down to free the strap of the camera bag. He was bewil-dered by her behavior, but his instincts told him that her agitation was directed at him and not the camera bag. He wasn't sure what he'd done to make her mad, but then he didn't really care either. "Jeez. If you're that eager to help, you can take that cooler too, honey."

Shocked by his rude and unchivalrous sugges-tion, she gasped as an angry fire began to lick at her insides. She picked up the cooler and stomped back to Colt's car, where he was releasing the latch on the trunk.

Trevor followed her.

"Where the hell did you learn sign language?" Colt asked Trevor, still flabbergasted when they met at the back of the car.

"Sesame Street." Colt looked startled, so Trevor

added, "Single mothers with little kids. I gotta do something while the coffee's brewing, so I watch T.V. with the kids. They have deaf people on that show, and I saw them do that once. It stuck in my head for some reason. It's the only sign I know, actually."

Colt was very much relieved in a selfish sort of way. The times he had difficulty communicating with Hannah were very frustrating for him. Deep in his heart he didn't want anyone to communicate with her better than he could, much less his own brother. It was self-indulgent and unfair to have such thoughts, and he wasn't proud of them, but he couldn't deny them either.

"What is all this stuff?" Trevor asked Colt, setting part of his load on the ground to hand Colt the suitcases.

"I think some of it's to develop pictures with, and the rest of it is what she needs to take the pictures for that promo layout for the sponsors," he said, studying the best approach to fitting everything into the trunk.

"Who?" He glanced at Willie, the camera bag still clutched tightly in her hands.

"Hannah."

"Hannah's a photographer?"

His revelation and interest sounded very like shock and skepticism to Willie.

"She's deaf, not blind," she said in a barbed tone of voice. "And she happens to be a great photographer."

"I'm sure she is," he said, staring at her in utter amazement. Now convinced that she was angry with him, he racked his brain for the reason. She had the bluest eyes he'd ever seen. They were the same color as the wildflowers that grew in patches around the farm every spring . . . except when she was upset. Then they were even more blue and exciting, like rare and precious jewels. Her freckles were cute too—if you liked women with freckles, and he did. But this little Willie sure was prickly, he thought, and he couldn't help but wonder why.

She muttered something about *Sesame Street* as she thrust the bag into Colt's hand and then turned to walk away. Trevor moved to the other side of the car to watch her.

"Who is that?" he asked, his interest more than a little piqued.

"Willie Willis," Colt said, taking note of the look on his brother's face. "Hannah's friend, self-appointed body guard, and assistant. Be nice to her, will you."

Willie Willis, Hannah's friend, self-appointed body guard—though it was entirely unconscious—and assistant sat in the backseat of the Trans Am for the next two hours, seething with anger nearly every time Trevor opened his mouth.

And he was nice to her, just as Colt had asked him to be. When they stopped for gas, Trevor kindly and graciously offered to go into the Coast-to-Coast store and buy them all soft drinks.

"Would you like anything else while I'm in there?" he asked her, leaning through Hannah's window to watch her reaction. "A candy bar, or a hairbrush maybe?"

Shew-wee! He was fast becoming addicted to the rush of excitement he felt whenever she turned those frosty blue eyes on him. There was menace and danger in them that he couldn't resist courting. Why, it would have been like turning his back on the biggest and best race of a lifetime.

Outside Roanoke they turned south and passed through a town called Boones Mill before they turned off the highway onto a country road. Shortly after that they came to a white-fenced farm with a mailbox at the gate that read, "MCKINNON."

Hannah could see immediately that what Colt called the farm and what she had pictured in her mind from his descriptions of growing corn and apples on it as a youth were two different things entirely.

A huge white farmhouse with a broad wrap-around porch and red shutters stood at the top of a small knoll. The rooftops of two more big build-ings behind the hill and to the right of the house were visible, but neither one of them looked like a barn. The fields surrounding the house were cut and trimmed neatly, the driveway was freshly grav-eled. Nothing about the place spoke of hard times or financial struggles.

"How many car dealerships do you own, ex-actly?" she asked when the car came to a stop in front of the steps leading to the great white porch of the house. "And where are the cornfields and apple trees?"

Colt laughed.

"Long gone," he said. He looked out proudly at the tranquillity he'd created on the old family homestead. "This is where we come to hide and relax now. We're not farm boys anymore, but we do still have to pick apples from time to time. She wouldn't let us get rid of all of them," he said, referring to his mother. "There's an orchard be-hind the house still."

"Yeah," Trevor said, confirming Colt's story. "Now she says that if we want pies, we have to pick our own apples. In the old days they were about all we ate. Baked apples, fried apples, mashed apples, apple dumplings, apple cider . . ." He continued his apple litany as he squeezed out of the backseat of the car. He glanced up at the sound of the front door opening. "Ah, and here's the apple of our eye."

Colt and Trevor greeted their mother with bear hugs and kisses, the kind Hannah had never quite been able to extract from her own parents. Her mother, a reserved and constrained person, had shown her love with control and blanket protection, and her father, a quiet, gentle soul had hugged her quietly and gently in keeping with his nature. Colt's mother was made of a different cloth.

"You need a haircut," Hannah saw her scolding Trevor, pulling at the curly locks that barely slid into the collar of his shirt.

"Girls love my hair, Mama," he teased her. "They run their fingers through it and play with it all the time. Feel it. They say they love the way it feels. Soft as a baby's."

"I gave you that hair. I don't want to touch it, you nasty boy," she said, holding his cheeks in her hands, rubbing them affectionately before she released him.

Already informed by Colt over the phone of Hannah's hearing loss and her mastery of lipreading, she then turned to her. "You're Hannah."

There was a hug for her, too, before the woman set her at arms' length and studied her face intently. "I knew that when Colt finally brought a girl home to meet me, she'd be as pretty as you are."

Colt stood by beaming, proud of both his women and not at all embarrassed at having his feelings exposed to the present company. Hannah, however, felt shy and awkward and pleased and very much in the limelight. She said all the appropriate things while she blushed self-consciously, then turned to Willie, hoping Willie would rescue her, as any good friend would.

"This is Willie Willis," she said.

"Sure you are. Colt told me about you, too, dear. Welcome," she said, turning the smile her sons had inherited on Willie. "That's a most unusual name you have. Is it short for something else?"

"No, ma'am. It's just Willie," she said, taking her hug like a good little soldier.

"Your mother named you Willie Willis," Trevor said, sounding incredulous.

She turned the fire in her eyes on him, but didn't answer. He grinned and put her name on the mental panel of buttons he could push—along with her hair, other women, bragging, and Hannah—to get a rise out of her.

Having hugged them all, Mrs. McKinnon was now the official mother. She gave the boys orders to bring in the luggage and where to put it. She commanded the girls into the kitchen to keep her company while she prepared lunch, and gave them both small helpful jobs to do while they got acquainted.

A short while later, when the boys tried to escape to what they called the shop—the buildings behind the house—she drafted them into her service and sent them to fetch apples from the cooler in the basement for supper.

Hannah enjoyed watching them grouse and complain, and grinned when Colt winked at her. She liked everything about his farm. His mother, the sights and smells, the easy love and affection that filled the air. It was the atmosphere in which Colt and Trevor had learned to be accepting of all the things that weren't exactly perfect in the world and to cherish the things that were. It was where they had come to know that it was more important to value people because of who they were than what they were, and to love without reservation. And all they knew, whether it was conscious or simply ingrained in them, Hannah could feel. She felt accepted, valued for who she was, and loved without reservation.

But that didn't mean that her life was suddenly a bowl of cherries . . . or apples. On the contrary. More than before she wanted to please them and fit in.

Seeing that she couldn't hold them back any longer, and with lunch nearly ready, Mrs. McKinnon finally allowed her sons to take Hannah and Willie to the shop to show them around.

Hannah had come to understand that the shop was a sort of garage where their race cars were built and worked on between events. But again she had underestimated and applied normal conceptions to what she was understanding. This was no country gas station garage they had built in their backyard. It was a huge multimillion-dollar operation.

She'd seen from the kitchen window the big eighteen-wheel tractor-trailer with Mallini-McKinnon Motorsports written on the side, and asked about it as they walked the sloping path to the shop. Colt explained that it was used to haul the cars and extra equipment to and from the tracks.

Her first impression of the place was that it was noisy. She felt the sounds vibrating in the door when she held it open to pass through.

Her second memory imprint was of size. The "shop" was a forty-thousand-square-foot facility, the two buildings in actuality just one. There were nine or ten cars under the larger of the two roofs, in various stages of refinement or repair. Eighteen or more men were bent over, around, under, and on top of cars, working diligently.

And machinery. . . . There were tools, tires, and machinery *everywhere*. Not just wrenches and batteries and regulators either. Computerized machines with digital displays, electronic machines with paper printouts, sheet-metal cutters, riveters, hydraulic lifts, barometers, gauges, and much more she couldn't keep up with.

Colt led her by the hand into the shop to meet everyone. At first, because of the great noise, they didn't realize she was deaf. She would have put their discovery off a while longer, too, if the first man's name hadn't been Daryl Eslick.

"I'm sorry. I didn't catch that," she said.

Colt smiled regretfully, saying, "This'll take all day if I try to finger spell everything I don't know signs for. Would you mind if Willie translated for you?"

"No. Of course not."

Soon everyone in the shop knew she couldn't hear and that turning off the machinery wouldn't help. She was used to the varied reactions she received when people first discovered she was different. The questioning and pitying looks, the discomfort, the shouting and exaggerated speech. She was also accustomed to the feelings of frustration and failure she experienced when, more than anything, she wanted to fit in and become part of a group but couldn't.

Willie was having no such problems. She talked to the mechanics and asked questions. They were polite and friendly. Her problem was with Trevor, who insisted on following her around, bumping into her whenever she stopped and touching her arm whenever she stepped over something, as if she had two left feet and couldn't manage to do it herself.

What really irritated her was bending to look at something and having him pull her hair back, grazing her neck with his fingers, and having him tauntingly murmur into her ear, "You wouldn't want to get this caught. What a hairy mess that would be, huh?"

But for Hannah it was a time during which she felt extremely self-conscious of Colt's attention as he laboriously tried to explain the use and value of an English wheel to her with Willie's assistance. It would have been so much easier for him if she weren't deaf, she lamented. Men who were obviously his friends as well as his employees wouldn't be staring at them, wouldn't be wondering why he hadn't hired a hearing photographer in the first place.

That was when she met Frank Hoffman, Colt's crew chief. He was a big burly man in his fifties or maybe sixties who appeared to be as old and wise and as work-worn as the hills—and someone very important, by the appearance of things in the shop.

With great affection and pride, Colt introduced the older man to Hannah through Willie.

He grinned. "You're deaf!" he exclaimed. "Wait a second, let me think here a minute. Oh, yeah." He signed, "Pleased to see you," and then his grin got bigger, if that was possible.

Hannah wanted to cry, or at least reach out and hug the old man. Here was another accepting soul. And where there was one, there eventually came another.

"I'm happy to meet you," she said sincerely.

"Oh, you talk. That's good," he said, meaning no insult, simply speaking his opinion. "Makes things a little easier anyway, huh? I got a niece who's deaf, but she won't talk. At least you can scream and cuss when you're mad, and you don't have to stop when your arms get tired."

She hadn't really thought of it in those terms, but he was right. She laughed and turned to Colt. "Don't get any ideas about turning me in for a nonspeaking deaf girl."

He was taken aback until he saw that she was teasing him. "Where the hell were you when I was falling in love with this one?" he asked, glaring at Frank Hoffman. "You could have told me there were quieter ones."

The rest of the time they spent in the shop was actually tolerable. There was still some awkwardness, and several times she took pictures of things that were supposed to be secret, putting this or that mechanic in a tizzy, but Colt was there to help and to smooth ruffled feathers. He told the men to let her have a free shot at everything, because he had first and final option on all the pictures.

Frank and a man who built engines, Jerry Wilks, joined them for lunch at Mrs. McKinnon's table. She served sandwiches, cold fried chicken, mashed potatoes, and several different salads, all the while teasing and force-feeding everyone in turn.

Colt was supremely happy. Hannah was a hit with the important people in his life, and more importantly, she was comfortable with them.

"Please," she said quietly several minutes into the meal. "I'm very interested in what everyone is saying, but I'm having a hard time keeping up with the conversation. I can't tell who's talking or what you're saying if you don't look at me. Would you mind if Willie signed for me?"

No one minded, of course, but it filled Colt's heart with pride and satisfaction that she felt relaxed enough among them to ask. It pleased him, too, to see the chairs around the table gradually turning in Hannah's direction, and the subtle hand movements and body language his family was beginning to use, consciously or not, to make it easier for her to see who was speaking and what was being said.

"I'm going to Martinsville this afternoon," Trevor said casually, looking at Colt. "Want to come?"

Hannah could see tension passing from one person to the next around the table. There was a look on Colt's face that she couldn't read. He lowered his eyes from Trevor's, glanced at her briefly, then shook his head.

"No. I have a few things I need to get done in the office this afternoon," he said. Then, looking at Hannah again, he added, "Trevor's taking a car over to the Martinsville track for a few test laps. Would you like to go with him?"

"Yes, I would. I'd like to go back to the shop for a

few more pictures, too, but I can do that tomorrow morning. That is, if everyone will be back tomorrow," she said.

Frank Hoffman said something and everyone laughed, then he spoke to her more directly. "My crew works seven days a week, eight or ten hours a day, or they don't work for me. They'll be there any old time you want to visit the shop, sweet thing."

"How about you, sweet thing?" Trevor asked Willie, using Frank's endearment for Hannah like a candied harpoon on Willie. "Wanna see me in action?"

"No." She looked at Hannah. "You won't need me, will you?"

"I don't think so," she said. "But are you sure you don't want to see this? I think it'll be fun."

"I'd rather have a tooth pulled," she muttered.

"Awk." Trevor groaned, slapping a hand over his heart. "Stop. My ego can't take this. Mama, Willie's being mean to me."

Mrs. McKinnon passed her hand under the table to pat Willie's knee. "I'm sure she has her reasons, dear."

Willie's face turned bright red under her freckles.

"I can't think of one," he said, looking mortally wounded. "I've been trying to charm her pants off all morning, and she's been nothing but nasty."

"Maybe you've lost your touch, sport," Colt suggested, winking at Willie. "Maybe she finds you totally resistible."

"Me?" He looked long and hard at her, her blue eyes flashing storm warnings, her pink lips pouting. Finally he said, "Nah. I think she's playing hard to get."

Seven

In the end it was Hannah alone who accompanied Trevor and a few members of the crew to the half-mile track south of Martinsville. Tuesdays weren't prime racing time. For a fee and with arrangements to have a rescue squad unit standing by on the field, the track was theirs for the afternoon.

With seating for twenty-one thousand spectators, the oval asphalt track with its boxwoods growing neatly along the turns was an impressive sight to a novice like Hannah. Racetracks were a lot bigger than they looked on television, not that she'd seen that much of them before she'd swiftly changed channels. She wasn't sure what she'd been expecting, but the size and potential filled her with wonder and anticipation.

She stood under the hot sun while they released the Mallini-McKinnon Pontiac from the short trailer. Mallini-McKinnon because they owned the car; Pontiac because with a broad stretch of the imagination it resembled a late-model Pontiac with gross modifications. It was bright yellow with a lucky number eleven on the door and decals representing everything from lumber to refrigeration to hygiene products stuck everywhere else.

Trevor took the track at a reasonable pace the first time around, blowing a cloud of dark smoke like a tail behind him. But once he'd burned the excess oil off the engine, his speed picked up and up and up. The ground under Hannah's feet trembled when he whizzed past her, and before she could blink, he'd passed her again, taking her breath away.

She missed most of what was being said, the mechanics being too busy and too engrossed in the car to pay her any attention. But she didn't need words to pick up on the energy and excitement they were feeling. It was serious business, but it was more than that. It was their lifeblood, the sparkle in their lives. It was what they did to give their hearts wings.

Her hands balled into fists and her nails dug into her palms as she watched Trevor zoom around and around, faster and faster, until he was practically a blur. So close, so close, she thought over and over before she realized what she was feeling. Trevor was touching death, taunting it, pushing himself and the car as close as he could, tickling it, never quite stepping over the boundary. He's crazy, she told herself even as part of her envied his nerve.

When he finally pulled into the infield, he was sweating and grinning like a fool. She couldn't help it, she smiled too.

The crew was all over the car in a matter of seconds, and Hannah stood back out of their way. Trevor squeezed out of the window in the door and stood talking to Frank for a few minutes before he swaggered over to her.

"What do you think?"

"It's wonderful. Scary, but wonderful. And you're

crazy," she said, knowing he'd take it as a compliment.

"Not really." He sobered enough to let her know he was serious. "I'm very careful. That car's safer at two hundred miles an hour than yours is at fifty-five on the highway. We're not out there trying to kill ourselves, Hannah. We're just racing."

"Can I feel it?"

"What? The car?" he asked, confused. "Sure. All you want."

"No. I mean, would you start the engine again so I could feel it?"

Without an answer he walked back to the car, climbed in, and turned the starter. Hannah placed both her hands on the hood, snatching them back quickly when it burned her. Trevor sent her a grimace of apology and motioned to one of the mechanics. He stepped forward and gave her a greasy rag.

Through the rag on the hood she could feel the power in the engine. It shook through her arms and into her shoulders. There was enough force under the hood of the car to lift an airplane off the ground.

She grinned at Trevor, wondering what it must be like to control something of such might, wondering what it would be like to feel the power in her hands, direct it. . . . She bit her lower lip as her next thought took form.

Trevor was reading her mind, or maybe he was simply relating to the expression on her face. Either way, they stared at each other for a decisive second or two before he let loose his woman-killing grin and nodded.

He lifted himself from the car, calling orders she couldn't make out, then walked to the front of the car.

"You don't have a NASCAR license, but I won't tell if you don't." He grinned at her. "Now there won't be anyone else on the track, so all you have to concentrate on is the road in front of you," he said, making sure that she understood every word he was saying. "Don't go any faster than you feel comfortable with. Don't slam on the brakes unless you have to. Ease your foot off the gas first and let it slow by itself, then use the brakes if it's necessary." He paused to make that clear. "Slow down on the curves. You can go faster on the straightaways, but slow on the curves. Got that?"

She nodded as one of the men handed her a pair of Nomex overalls. She stepped into them and zipped up the front. Trevor put his hand on her shoulder to get her attention again.

"We won't be able to talk to you through this," he said, placing his helmet with its built-in two-way radio down over the top of her head. "But we'll leave it on in case you want to talk to us." He bent to roll the legs of the fireproof suit up a little, as it was too big for her, then started in on the sleeves. "We'll use that chalkboard there to communicate with you, so watch for it. Okay?"

"Yes."

"Ready?"

"Yes," she said, feeling the quiver in her voice.

Her knees felt a little weak as she walked to the driver's side of the car. With her hand on the side panel she could feel that the car had been left running, waiting for her. She tried to swallow the thick lump of fear in her throat, but it was stuck hard and fast.

Trevor lifted her from behind with both arms and stepped back so that she could lower herself into the seat feet first. He leaned through the window and fastened her seat belt, showed her the speedometer and tachometer, and instructed her to watch the oil pressure gauge. He gave her a pair of gloves and backed out of the window, knocking twice on her helmet.

She looked at him, and he gave her a thumbs-up sign and a good-luck smirk. Frank Hoffman whacked the hood of the car and did the same. For a moment she was tempted to crawl out from behind the thick rubber tubes and metal bars and forget the whole thing, but . . .

Colt heard the horns and war whoops before the van and trailer reached the drive. It was nearly suppertime. He stood on the porch and watched as the van—looking as if it had grown arms and legs through the side windows—billowed dust up through the gravel drive in its hurry to get to the front porch.

"Whoa, Colt," bellowed Trevor, stepping out of the van the instant it came to a complete stop. "You should have seen her! She was the wind. Lightning. She was incredible!" he said, the crew backing his words with loud, jubilant words of their own. He lifted Hannah from the van to dance her around in circles before swinging her feet to the ground. "You should have seen her."

Willie stepped out of the house to join Colt on the porch.

"You should have come, sweet thing," Trevor said with an eat-your-heart-out smirk for the freckle-faced blonde. "I could have given you the thrill of your life too."

She grimaced at him.

Colt leaned against a tall white pillar watching Hannah. She was windblown and flushed with excitement, her eyes bright and shimmering. She was so unbelievably beautiful to him that he almost forgot to comment on his crew's good spirits.

"You got all her bugs ironed out then," he said, sparing them a momentary glance before his gaze returned to Hannah.

"Bugs?" Trevor asked. Comically he started

weeding through Hannah's hair. "This girl don't have a bug on her, brother."

"Colt," Hannah said, running toward him. "It was wonderful. At first I thought I was going to die of fright, but then it got exciting and—"

Her words came to an abrupt halt as she took the first step and looked up into Colt's face. It wasn't Colt's face anymore. It was a visage of rage and agony unlike any she'd ever seen before. Unlike anything human. Directed not at her but over her shoulder at Trevor.

She gasped when he leaped from the porch, pinning Trevor to the front of the van before she could turn around. His emotions shook both men physically, and the unmasked fear in Trevor's face brought terror to her heart.

"Colt, no," she cried out, but he couldn't seem to hear her through his anger. For long seconds he held his brother immobile, confronting his fury, then in a flash of sanity he jerked himself loose of his brother's shirtfront and stalked off in the direction of the shop, leaving the entire company pale and dazed.

Dinner was . . . strained. Not the big pot roast Mrs. McKinnon had spent the afternoon cooking, but the atmosphere around it. She was tactful and polite like a diplomat who knew that tempers had to calm before a reasonable reconciliation could come about.

Trevor was sullen and speechless. There were fleeting, probing glances in his brother's direction as if he wanted to approach him, wanted to make amends, but didn't know how.

Even Willie was uncomfortable and silent, confused by the incident. She knew when to stay out of a bad situation though, and didn't ask any questions.

Hannah was perhaps the most miserable person at the table. She was the cause of the altercation between the brothers. She was the one who had wanted to drive the car. It had been her idea, not Trevor's. She felt awful about the whole thing.

She was also peeved at Colt. He had no right in the world to tell her what she could and couldn't do—she'd assumed they'd settled that point when they'd finally agreed she'd go to the tracks to take pictures for the project. Obviously they hadn't. She was hell-bent on establishing a few ground rules between her and Colt before their relationship went any further. But first she felt she ought to do something to repair the damage she'd caused in the relationship between the two brothers.

In order to do that, she had to get Colt to talk to her. She felt sure that if he knew she'd been scared witless during the entire affair, and that she hadn't driven the car any faster than eighty miles an hour—a snail's pace compared to the speeds at which Trevor drove—he'd feel better and perhaps more forgiving. But he wasn't giving her a chance to tell him.

He'd returned to the house about twenty minutes after the scuffle in the front yard and had gone straight to his room on the second floor. Hannah had cleaned up for dinner and changed her clothes to give his temper time to settle before she went to him. She had knocked on his door twice, but he hadn't opened it. On the off chance that he'd called for her to come in, she'd tried the doorknob and found it locked. He'd appeared for dinner a few minutes later, outwardly calm but still a striking image of a man exerting a great deal of effort to keep a lid on his emotions.

Colt knew better. If he appeared to have himself temporarily under control, he was a better actor than his brother ever thought of being. His composure was tenuous at best, and he was living in mortal fear that he'd lose it. Every time he thought of what he'd come so close to doing to his brother, he shuddered.

It wasn't Trevor's fault that Colt was a coward. Letting Hannah drive the car had been stupid, but knowing Hannah, Colt realized that Trevor wouldn't have been able to refuse her. There was an apology deep in Colt's soul, but his pride refused to release it. Trevor knew him better than anyone. Trevor knew what was inside of him; he'd seen Colt's weaknesses before. Colt simply couldn't bear for Trevor to see them again.

And Hannah? He couldn't even look Hannah in the eye. Dear Lord. If he had half her courage, he could call himself a man again. Every time she turned around she faced her fears and met them head on. She had more fortitude than she had common sense, in his opinion, but at least she *had* fortitude, he thought in self-contempt. How could he ask her to love a man who couldn't confront his own fears?

"Colt?" Her voice came softly into his private hell. "Colt, it wasn't Trevor's idea."

He barely glanced at her as he stood away from the table and put out a halting hand.

"Please," he said. "Could we talk about this later, Hannah? Right now . . . I . . . can't. Excuse me."

She slumped back in her chair as she watched him leave the room. She looked around at the morose faces at the table, her gaze lingering on the sadness in Mrs. McKinnon's expression.

"I'm sorry, Mrs. McKinnon," she said. "I didn't mean for this to happen."

The older woman covered Hannah's hand with her own and gave it a gentle squeeze. "You haven't done anything to be sorry for, dear."

"No. I have. I know Colt worries about me. I shouldn't have put Trevor in such an awkward position," she said, looking to Trevor. "I'm sorry, Trevor."

With his chin on his fist he looked back at her and shook his head. "It's not you, Hannah. You haven't done anything wrong." He hesitated, glanced at his mother, and then seemed to make up his mind about something. He stood, saying, "Come on, Hannah. You need to know about this."

Bewildered, she followed him through the living room, down the hall, and into a room that must have been an office, but looked more like a trophy room. Mrs. McKinnon and Willie followed them into the room at a discreet distance.

There were pictures everywhere. So many that there was no evidence of the color of the walls. And trophies, a hundred perhaps, were scattered on shelves and lined up on the floor.

"Colt calls this his office," Trevor said. "But it's more like his torture chamber."

Sure that she'd misunderstood his words, Hannah turned to Willie for help.

The girl finger-spelled the words for her by reflex, keeping a discerning eye on Trevor.

Torture chamber? It made no sense. The room was filled with prizes for past achievements, happy memories, and souvenirs. She began to look more closely, searching for anything that would cause Colt pain.

The trophies came in a variety of sizes and shapes and were evenly divided between the brothers, with Trevor's name engraved on the bottom as many times as Colt's—even though he hadn't been racing as long.

The pictures were an insult to her artistic eye, but they were interesting nonetheless. Nearly every one had a car in it. She skipped the photos of cars alone and moved on to those of Colt leaning against one with a cheeky grin and one foot braced on the front bumper . . . or of Trevor in the same position . . . or of both of them as boys in the same position with an older man in the middle, an arm around each of them.

"Your father?" she asked, knowing the answer without the nod of Trevor's head.

They'd inherited their smiles from their mother, but the rest of them had been cloned from their father. The tall, lean body with the easy I-worked-for-everything-I've-got-so-I-know-it's-mine stance that she'd admired the first night she'd seen Colt on the balcony had come from their father. The lines around Colt's eyes told of understanding and humor, and those around Trevor's revealed mischief and amusement. There was no denying that each son had received something distinct and different from his father.

Hannah maneuvered herself along the wall, lingering on pictures of the brothers in more recent years. There was another young man in these, a handsome young man with serious eyes that belied the wide, fun-loving grin on his lips. Slightly shorter and older than both Colt and Trevor, this third man was in nearly as many photos as their father, and was just as easy to pick out.

"Who is this man?" she asked, curious.

"Joe Mallini," Trevor said.

"Oh, yes. Your partner. Colt said the three of you are like brothers," she said, looking more closely at the man in the photograph. "I'm anxious to meet him."

A few seconds passed before she felt Trevor's hand on her arm.

"Hannah, you're not going to meet Joey," he said. There was a void in his eyes, an empty space it seemed, between the moment they were sharing and a distant pain. "He's dead."

"Oh. I thought that with his name all over everything that . . . I didn't know."

"Colt won't drop the Mallini name. It helps keep his pain alive."

"What pain? I don't understand."

"Colt killed Joey five years ago."

"What?" She automatically turned to Willie for a correct translation, not believing her eyes.

Trevor took her arm again.

"It was an accident. It could have been anyone. Joey was just out of the pit. On the second lap he took a spin coming out of the sharp curve at Martinsville. Colt was at the head of the pack and took him head on. It could have been anyone. I was there. It could have been me. But . . . he . . . he says he saw him, Joey's face, before he hit him."

Hannah was numb and sick at once. She wanted to empathize with Colt, but she couldn't begin to imagine what it must have been like. She couldn't conceive the horror of its happening or the agony and misery that must have followed. It was too horrible for her to comprehend. She stood there, heartsick, wanting to cry for Colt's sake but unable to do so. Somehow it just didn't seem real.

"He wouldn't sleep in the hospital. And . . ."

"The hospital?" she asked, overwhelmed and feeling a bit muddled. Willie had moved to a position behind and to one side of Trevor to cue Hannah to what he'd been saying. For an instant she looked as lost as Hannah felt.

"The accident totaled both cars. Colt broke his leg." He leaned back against the desk top and folded his arms across his chest defensively, as if doing so would protect his heart from the past as he recalled the details. "I lay on the track, on my belly, talking to Colt, trying to keep him still while they cut him out of his car. Joey died instantly, but Colt . . . He's been dying ever since." He glanced at her with a tiny smile on his lips. "Until you came along. You're good for him, Hannah. Maybe you can help him deal with this."

She shook her head. "I don't know. I can't even picture it in my mind." No one spoke for long, endless minutes. Then she asked, "What happened at the hospital?"

"Oh," Trevor said, as if being pulled back to the moment from some faraway place. "Well, Colt wouldn't sleep. Every time he tried he woke up screaming. He'd see Joey's face in his dreams. It was months—a year, huh, Mama?—before he could sleep the night through without waking up in a cold sweat."

A sad, melancholy look took command of his features, and he began to speak as if he were alone with his thoughts. "I miss Joey, but I miss Colt more. He was always at the point, in everything. Everything he did, he did full tilt. I mean, I'm good, but he was so much better. Dad used to say that Colt didn't have a nerve in his body, and that's why he could race the way he did. Didn't he used to say that, Mama?"

"Yes, dear," she said, silent tears rolling down her cheeks for both her sons.

"I drive my ass off to win for him," he said in a feeble attempt at anger and frustration. "And all he'd have to do to win is drive the damn car himself."

He fell silent, into a place where no one else was invited to join him, and the women lowered their eyes, respecting his privacy and seeking places of their own in which to hide their thoughts.

Well, Hannah and Mrs. McKinnon did. Willie wasn't much of a hider, and she didn't feel like respecting Trevor's private thoughts. She wanted him to share them with her. She wanted him to let her pick them apart and analyze them, discover their origins. This was a side of Trevor McKinnon that few if any women aside from his mother had seen before. And it was very appealing. More so than his smile or the twinkle in his eyes. More than his playfulness and his blatant and well-advertised sexual charm. This was a Trevor McKinnon that a woman could sink her hooks into and come away with something real in her hands. And Willie planned to do just that.

"Is . . . Is this why Colt stopped racing?" Hannah asked, putting the bits and pieces of Colt's life into place. "Not because the business got too big, but because of the accident?"

A chuckle escaped him as he suddenly stood and walked to the door. It was as if he'd spent enough time in the past and had to leave.

"Well, the company has doubled in size," he said, flicking off the light switch as he passed through, leaving the women to follow him out of the darkness. "But that wasn't until after the accident and Colt started driving himself crazy looking for things to keep his mind occupied." He laughed aloud then. "Remember the year he wanted to buy that fast-food chain, Mama? I thought he was going to drive me nuts with that one. I finally went out and begged the competitors to be our sponsors."

"And that stopped him?" Willie asked, thinking it a strange tactic, not understanding the influence of sponsorship on the sport of auto racing.

"Sure did," he said, spreading his long form across one end of the couch in the living room. "He may not race anymore, but it's in his blood. And he's every bit as good an owner as he was a driver. Last year he let it slip out that we were looking to take on a second team for the Grand Nationals because I was going for the Winston Cup. Man, it was no time at all before he had sponsors crawling all over him, offering him money."

"Doesn't that put a lot of pressure on you to win?" Willie asked with a new and sudden interest in racing.

"No more than I put on myself," he said. "You're either racing to win or you're not. You give it your best and that's all you can do. No, the only problem with sponsors is all the extra stuff you've got to do to keep them happy. PR pictures. This *event,* that *event.* Dumb stuff like . . . tellin' people that if stock cars were made of wood, you *personally* would choose so-and-so's lumber to build it, or swearin' on national T.V. that you'd rather let your head explode than take anything but your sponsor's product for your headache, stuff like that." He was thoughtful, then added, "Course, I don't really mind all the things you get to do with the pretty girls."

"Of course not," Willie said.

Willie went on to say more, but Hannah's attention began to wander—around the corner, up the stairs, and through the door into Colt's room. She had no idea what she could or would say to him, but she felt an overpowering need to be with him. To hold him. To love him.

Not to love him in the sense that a woman loves a man, she cautioned herself. But love him in the person-caring-for-another-person way. She wanted to comfort and soothe him if she could. She just wanted to be with him.

That other sort of love, the man-woman kind . . . well, she felt it. She did love him. But it was too early for the telling and they had a lot to work out between them before they could make any commitment, she thought prudently.

A hearing person living with a deaf person wasn't something that either could enter into lightly. Even her own father said it was frustrating. She wanted to be sure of Colt before she offered him her heart, and he needed to know all there was to know about her before he could be sure.

It wasn't easy, this falling-in-love business, she thought. Especially for people from different worlds. Just thinking about it wore her out.

She looked across the room at Mrs. McKinnon, who sat in a rocking chair knitting and smiling while she eavesdropped on Willie and Trevor's conversation. Hannah's gaze moved across the coffee table to her friend and Colt's brother. Trevor was teasing her again. Hannah could tell by the irritation in Willie's face.

"If you'll excuse me," she said, truly tired and too keyed up and worried about Colt to stay and amuse herself with their banter, "I think I'll go up to bed now. Thank you for having me, Mrs. McKinnon."

"It's good having you here, dear," Mrs. McKinnon said, smiling her sincerity. "Sleep well."

Trevor had unfolded himself from the couch to stand next to her. When she turned to say good night, he stopped her.

"Hannah. About what happened this afternoon. It wasn't your fault. It was the track. He hasn't been back to it since the accident, not even to watch practice runs," he said. "He might have been a little peeved that I let you drive the car at all, but he's been mad at me before." He shrugged and smiled as if Colt's anger alone wouldn't have changed what he'd done. "It was you on that particular track that set him off this afternoon."

"I understand," she said, patting his chest affectionately. "I just wish we hadn't hurt him."

She went to her room and got ready for bed, but she couldn't sleep. She wanted to. She wanted to push the day's events out of her mind, forget what she'd been told and exist blissfully in her dreams of being held in Colt's arms the way she had been the night before.

It was a while before she noticed the restless ache in her body and began to wonder if it was wise for Colt to be alone in his room and what exactly it was that he was doing in there all by himself. More time passed before she could work up the mettle to face the consequences of disturbing him. He might send her away. But she was willing to accept whatever repercussions she had to, just to see him.

She tucked the short cotton robe closely around the big athletic T-shirt and panties she used for warm-weather sleeping, then opened her door. The upstairs hall was empty. There was no light shining from under any of the doors, but there was a low glowing light from the foyer below that dispelled the darkness enough to allow her to walk unimpeded to Colt's door.

She tapped lightly and, getting no response, gritted her teeth and tried it again, unsure of how much noise she was making. Still no response. She wasn't sure how Mrs. McKinnon would feel about her guests room-hopping in the middle of the night, and she thought about waiting until morning to talk to Colt—but she didn't want to. She needed to see him. She needed to be with him.

"Colt?" she said, putting a strain on her voice in the hopes of decreasing its volume, cringing at the thought that it probably wasn't anywhere near a whisper. "Colt? It's Hannah."

Still no answer.

"Colt? If you just told me to get lost, you're going to have to open the door and say it to my face, you know."

She waited for him to do exactly that, but nothing happened.

"Colt. I like your mother, and I don't want her to think I'm some hussy sneaking around in the dark trying to seduce her son. Open the door before she catches me out here," she said, praying to God that she didn't sound as if she were talking through a megaphone. A quick glance up and down the hall told her she was safe from discovery for the moment, but she was getting nervous and impatient. She kicked the door with her bare foot.

"Ouch! dammit, Colt, open the door. I won't leave until you tell me to go away."

She was bouncing on one foot, holding her big toe in both hands, when she felt a hand on her shoulder. She screamed in fright, turned, and threw her back against Colt's door.

"Ah," she cried weakly. "You scared me to death."

"Sorry," Colt said. He didn't look sorry. He was chuckling at her.

"I thought you were in your room."

"So I heard." He laughed, enjoying himself considerably more than she was. "My mother likes you, too, and she doesn't think you're a hussy."

"I can't see what you're saying," she said in a fluster. Mortified, she made a face and looked down the hall, convinced that everyone in the house must have heard her. He was grinning with that look she liked to think he gave only to her when he reached behind her and opened his bedroom door, using his other hand to push her gently into the brighter light within.

It wasn't the little boy's room she'd been expecting to see, the one his loving mother preserved with care. It was a man's bedroom with big, heavy furniture, brass lamps, light-color walls and thick drapes at the windows. A master bedroom with an adjoining bathroom and walk-in closets. Not a teenager's room where sex was forbidden except in his mind or when his parents were out of town. It was a man's room where nothing he did in it, illicit or not, was anyone's business but his own.

Somehow it didn't make Hannah any more comfortable.

"Are you all right?" she asked, pretending that she'd aroused the entire household just to check on him.

He nodded, as embarrassed and tense as she was but for different reasons. He'd never have her courage, but he didn't have to act like a madman.

He'd shown her his cowardice and felt shame deep in his soul. If he couldn't have her respect and love, he could at least ask for her forgiveness if he'd humiliated her as well.

"I'm sorry. . . ." he got out, but she quickly covered his lips with the tips of her fingers.

"No. I'm sorry," she said. "Not about driving the car. I'd have driven the car anyway. But I wouldn't have driven it on that track if I'd known how it would hurt you. I didn't mean to."

"I know," he said, realizing that she knew the whole story. He wasn't sure if he was glad to have it out in the open, or if he ought to punch Trevor in the mouth for telling her. "I am sorry I overreacted. I made a fool of myself . . . again."

"Not with me," she said, her low voice thick and husky with her emotions.

"You don't think I'm a coward?" he asked, convinced that she did.

"No." She followed him as he walked across the thick, dark carpet to sit on the edge of the bed. "I think you're a kind, gentle man who's been forced to live through something so awful that I can't even begin to comprehend it."

He glanced at her but wouldn't hold her gaze, sure that if their positions were reversed, she would have had the courage to come to grips with it and handle it better.

They sat side by side on the bed for long seconds before Hannah asked, "What was Joey Mallini like?"

Colt couldn't answer. He'd never put who Joey was into words before.

"He was . . . a good man," he started. After those few words, more rushed to his lips. Like water through an old crack in a dike, his memories trickled through slowly. Then, as the crack grew larger, they flowed in a steady stream.

Hannah followed him when he lay back on the

bed with one elbow under his head. She propped herself up to watch him speak, missing some of it occasionally, but not really caring so long as he continued to talk with a look of happy remembrances on his face.

She lost all feeling in her wrist as he told her stories and humorous anecdotes about Joe Mallini into the wee hours of the morning. A cool breeze found its way in through the open window, and they crawled under the light covers, supporting themselves with pillows without missing a beat in Colt's story.

The catalog of Joey Mallini's life wound down to the night of the race at Martinsville, when Colt glanced at Hannah and found her half asleep, her expression dull and drowsy.

"You are so beautiful," he said, smoothing her hair away from her face with one hand. Beautiful to look at, yes, but even more beautiful to be with, he thought, adoring her with his eyes.

"What?" she asked, his new expression catching her unawares.

"I love you," he said.

Uh-oh, she thought. "You hardly know me."

"I know all I need to know about you."

"No," she said, wary and wanting to distract him. "You only think you know me. I've been pretty nice to you"—she drew her hand slowly up the front of his shirt—"and you're infatuated with me"—she felt his hand press her breast firmly—"and my good looks. All I've shown you is my good side. I have a bad side, too, you know."

"You do?" His interest was aroused. He pulled at the knot in her sash, saying, "Well, do you consider being stubborn and obstinate good or bad?"

She smiled. "Good."

He freed the edges of her robe and pushed it open to slide his hands under her T-shirt.

"What about someone who has no idea what it is

to stay out of harm's way, who flaunts danger in fact. What about them? Would that be part of their good side or their bad side?"

"You mean like race car drivers?" she asked, laughing at his expression when he saw his error. "Good." But then thinking about it, she added, "I think."

"Do you think it's a good quality in a photographer?" He waited until she saw his question before he buried his face in her soft, sweet-smelling hair, then began to nibble on the tender flesh at her neck, his hands burning a path up her ribs as they pushed her T-shirt away.

"Well, ah, if the man the photographer's . . . ah . . . working for is too . . . too protective, then it sort of . . . evens out in the end. Ah. . . . Doesn't it?"

If he answered, she wasn't aware of it. She closed her eyes against the low lamplight and let his hands and gentle kisses weave a rapturous darkness about her.

Later. When the stars and the moon were once again in their rightful places in the sky, and the planets had resumed their timeless orbits around the sun, and the lovers lay replete and relaxed in each other's arms, Colt reached out and turned out the light.

He rolled back in the bed, his arms falling loosely about Hannah's shoulders and waist, and he sighed. Had any woman ever felt so good in his arms before? he wondered, dozing, his mind free-floating in the space between sleep and wakefulness. Had any woman ever made him feel so good, period?

Her image filled his mind like the sun filled the sky at dawn. She brought hope and promise into his heart. She spread a balm of peace and joy over the loneliness in his soul. She gave a purpose to everything in his life. Memories of other women faded away to a blink in time. Recollections of the past were distant and insignificant, his yesterdays beginning anew on the night they'd met.

Even Joe Mallini's death took on a dreamlike quality that made it seem unreal. Well, not unreal, but . . . over somehow. He'd tried to cleave to his pain and sorrow as he talked about Joey earlier, but it kept slipping away. It was as if each word of remembrance that he'd given to Hannah snapped one of the tight, biting coils that had kept his anguish raw and bleeding for so many years.

He breathed in deeply of Hannah's scent and plunged deeper into sleep thinking he could actually feel his wounds closing and healing. Visions of the track at Martinsville came to him. Not ghoulish or sinister visions, but hot, bright, and sunny ones, as they had been when he was young. Hannah was there, looking beautiful. Motors roared in his ears like a symphony of music. He felt power in his hands, and his shoulders tensed with an exhilarating strength to contain it. His heart raced with joy and excitement. He was driving again.

Eight

The weeks that followed Hannah's visit to the McKinnon farm were busy, hectic, and splendid. The happiest Hannah had ever known.

There was still a lot of catalog work to do, and her agent, Peter Watson, was becoming insistent about an answer for a showing at the Merritt Gallery, but these tasks could be performed and ignored in turn, with Colt ever-present in the back of her mind to take away the monotony and to swallow up her fears. She found she could do anything during the day, when she had nights with Colt to look forward to.

He was making strides in his study of sign language. Most of it was on-the-job training, with both Hannah and Willie showing him how best to convey his thoughts. He seemed amazed that so few signs said so much. He was still slow and jerky, but every night he'd come to her with two or three new gestures committed to memory from a book, and he retained all that he'd learned before.

It wasn't just sign language he was learning, though. He was discovering what it was to truly love a deaf person. He'd spent an entire afternoon angry as hell because he'd realized he had no way of contacting her to tell her that he'd be late for their date except to drive over to her house. He'd finally resorted to calling Gary Sherwin's office to get the number she used for her business, only to leave a message on a recorder in the hope that Willie would get the message to Hannah sometime before he arrived an hour late for their dinner. After that he carried the number of a relay service in his wallet and had TDD's installed in his office and then in his home. She *wasn't* a cheap date.

Movies and music were other things he learned about the hard way. She could share neither with him unless the movies were closed-captioned and the music was loud enough for her to feel the vibrations. She didn't begrudge him his car radio or even care when he brought home a movie that was over ten years old and not closed-captioned. She had long ago accustomed herself to these things. She would sit beside him, content in her silence just to be with him, and occupy herself some other way.

But Colt felt strange, and that was exactly what she wanted. He needed to get used to the idea that it was okay for him to hear what she couldn't. He needed to come to terms with his feelings as he began to understand that they could share their thoughts and feelings and opinions, that they could share visual beauty and touches and laughter—the important things in life. But there were many equally important things that they could never share with each other, and he needed to know that too.

Over and over he told her that he loved her. And she knew that he wanted to hear her say that she loved him too. But *she* needed to make it absolutely clear to him that even though their love was a wondrous, incredible thing, it wasn't going to be all cotton candy and Ferris wheels.

What made those weeks splendid, despite Hannah's misgivings, was Colt himself. He *was* learning and adjusting and accepting life with Hannah. Hannah the woman. Hannah the deaf person. Hannah the ambitious photographer.

By mid-July Hannah had attended eight big races in North and South Carolina, Florida, Delaware, New Hampshire, Georgia, and Tennessee. The empty half-mile track at Martinsville had in no way prepared her for what was to come. The tracks got bigger; seating capacity doubled, and the stands overflowed at race time. It became the crew's favorite pastime to terrify Hannah with stories of the even bigger tracks and larger crowds in the Winston Cup series.

The drivers and crew kept a hectic pace during the racing season. They traveled to their destination on Wednesday, practiced on Thursday, had time trials on Friday, raced on Saturday, and then traveled home for repairs and new equipment on Sunday.

Depending on their schedules, Colt, Hannah, and Willie flew together from Richmond to whatever airport got them closest to the track, and rented a car for the rest of their journey. These trips were especially fun when Trevor could join them.

"Is this humidity affecting your hair?" he'd ask Willie with his best Donahue impersonation. "It seems . . . bigger than usual."

She'd release a long-suffering sigh, and say, "How odd, so does your ego. Does it hurt when it's all puffed up and swollen like that?"

"Other swollen parts of me hurt more. Want me to show you where?"

"And risk catching some social disease? No, thank you."

The two of them had no kind words for each other. It had become the way of things between them. So it hadn't surprised anyone when Trevor, still superenergized and wobble-kneed from a race, had caught sight of Willie standing near the pit wall and suddenly scooped her up in his arms to plant an energetic kiss smack on her lips. That was simply Trevor. Nor had it shocked anyone when she gut-punched him. That was simply Willie.

The tracks were dirty and hot. They smelled of burnt rubber, popcorn, and exhaust. And they fairly breathed with a life of their own.

The Mallini-McKinnon team usually parked the big tractor-trailer transport in the infield, and it was there that the foursome split up to go their separate ways. The men to their assigned pit area with the cars and crew. The women, with their pit passes and crew jackets, out into the throng of spectators.

It was another of Colt's major accomplishments when he stopped trying to talk her out of wandering the speedways alone. At first he'd asked Willie to go with her, to watch over her and protect her, but she'd soon seen through this. Willie wasn't one to hide her boredom when there was nothing for her to do while Hannah took her pictures. They'd taken to separating once Colt was out of sight, but had made the mistake of returning to the transport separately—with Willie making her appearance first. "What if you don't hear a car coming up behind you?" he'd ranted at her when she'd insisted that she didn't need Willie to follow her around like a body guard. "What if some drunk tries to hit on you and won't take no for an answer? What if you get hit in the head with a lug wrench? A thousand things could happen to you here, Hannah. I won't be able to concentrate on the race, knowing that you're out in the crowd somewhere with no one to help you if you need it."

The discussion had continued for several more

minutes along this line before Hannah had finally
flipped her middle finger into the air at him and
stomped off to end it.

Colt's frown shifted from furious to curious. His
eyes narrowed suspiciously as he looked at Willie.
"Was that sign what I think it was, or . . ."

"No. I think that pretty much means the same
thing in any language," she said, grinning.

After that Colt had made one hard and fast rule
and then set her free. Hannah was to stay behind
the pit wall, which was most often a low pipe
railing or cinder-block retainer, before or during
the race, whether the car was in or not. No excep-
tions. If she fell over the wall trying to get a picture,
the crew was to throw her back, and *then* ask if
she was hurt.

He still worried about her. The expression on his
face when they kissed good-bye before each race
made that evident. But he didn't try and stop her
anymore. And Hannah didn't mind that he worried. Truth was, she liked it. She liked knowing
that he cared about her, that he was concerned for
her safety. There was nothing wrong with his
wanting to protect her, so long as he didn't try to
smother her.

And Hannah wasn't fool enough not to admit
that his fears were grounded in reality. The tracks
were dangerous, and especially so for a deaf person. Aside from the cars and the people that she
couldn't hear, there were any number of pitfalls
she could unwittingly fall into if she wasn't careful.
But she was careful when alone in the crowd.
Hannah was in her element.

She didn't need to hear or speak in a throng
of people. She could pretend she was invisible,
unseen, undetectable, and unimportant as she
passed among them taking pictures. As far as she
was concerned, it was the best part of the whole
assignment, her true calling.

People. Their faces. Their expressions. The locals and the out-of-towners. The three-piece suiters, the middle Americans, and the good ol' boys from the country. The way they carried their lives' stories in the curve and bend of their shoulders. The way they displayed their feelings in their actions and gestures. It was what Hannah loved best about people. Their unconscious honesty. She'd found that, like herself, other people were most alone in masses of their own kind.

They hid themselves, blended in, and let down their emotional defenses because they each thought they were just one of many, unnoticeable and safe. But they weren't any of those things to Hannah's camera. She passed among them taking candid shots of unguarded anger, envy, contentment, hate, joy, love, sorrow, pain, laughter, and zeal, showing the complexities of humanity, showing what made life a miracle.

The shots for Colt's project were fairly easy by comparison. She shot rolls of film of Trevor zooming by in the various bright-color Mallini-McKinnon Pontiacs. Some were modified for the short tracks, some for the speedways, and there were several alternates of both types. After the race, when she was finally allowed into the pit area, she shot several more rolls. Her triumph, however, how she truly earned the money Colt paid her, was in her humble opinion a stroke of sheer genius.

Like her one claim to fame—the cliff shots of Buzz Elliot—she wanted to show Trevor in the throes of what he did best. Riding with him during a race was out of the question. And she hadn't wanted to use a practice run to get the close ups, because the emotions wouldn't be as intense since there was nothing at stake.

No. She wanted the real thing. The exhilaration, the tension, the fear. And like the Buzz Elliot photos, she'd hit on a plan to get the pictures without endangering her life or Trevor's. She hadn't climbed that precipice of rock alongside Buzz as she had allowed Colt to assume at Gary Sherwin's office. She'd been lowered five or six feet over the side from the top in a metal basket attached to wire line connected to a hoist. It had been scary, but perfectly safe.

For Trevor she rigged up a camera inside the car—many of them had video cameras anyway. She used a great deal of time securing it at a good angle, just below the dashboard in front of him. It was a fully automated camera to which she attached a timer to shoot every sixty seconds. She had no choice but to use natural light, as a flash would have blinded him in the race, and there was no way of controlling the car's vibrations, but it would all be worth it if she got one good shot out of it.

The difficulty came in getting Frank Hoffman to agree to wasting precious pit time resetting the timer and reloading the camera. It was finally agreed upon that they'd do it three times during the three-hundred-mile race at Charlotte, and only when it wouldn't hold Trevor back. What more could she ask for?

Charlotte was also as good a place as any to take pit photos during the race. But since there were only six men allowed in the pit at one time, and they all had jobs to do and refused to give up any of their time to her—and, of course, since there was Colt's law about her being in the pit before or during the races—she had to find another way of getting photographs of the crew in action. Not back shots taken from the pit wall, which could be found in every book and magazine about racing that was ever published. Rather great shots that only Hannah Alexander could take.

As luck would have it, their pit at Charlotte was

located to the immediate right of the media center in the infield, which hovered some twenty or thirty feet off the ground, supported by an interesting array of beams and braces. To Hannah's way of thinking, it wasn't official "pit" territory, and if the braces could hold the weight of the press box, surely they could hold hers. . . .

Colt stood by—in no way idle, but not moving to stop her either—and watched with dread tight in his chest as the woman he loved climbed from one rotten-looking wooden brace to the next under the press box. Higher and higher. Twelve and then fourteen feet off the ground as the caution flag went out to the drivers, and the crew scurried to prepare for Trevor's next pit stop.

Through the radio headset Colt heard Trevor announce that he was feeling fine and on his way home for some milk and cookies. In other words, the car was running smoothly, and he was coming into the pit for gas and an outside tire change.

Colt held his breath and waited. Waited for the car to come in. Waited for the supports to give out under Hannah, for her to slip and fall. Waited for them to happen at the same time.

Trevor pulled the car in alongside the pit wall; the crew buzzed around it like bees in clover, and still Colt held his breath waiting for Hannah to lose her grip as she dangled from a support beam with one hand and clicked her camera furiously with the other.

Trevor was gone again, and Hannah was halfway down the support system under the press box when Colt's breath came bursting out again. It was full of colorful expletives as well as relief.

"Jeez." He spoke his thoughts aloud, pulling off his headset and wiping the sweat from his brow on his sleeve. "Doesn't anything scare her?"

"Everybody's afraid of something."

Colt turned to Willie, who stood beside the pile of

tires directly behind him. He eyed her curiously. She looked at him briefly and then looked away as if she wished she hadn't said anything.

He knew better than to try to quiz her about Hannah. She'd already shown him how fiercely loyal she was the night they'd met in Virginia Beach. Even now she looked as if she'd rather have her tongue nailed to the floor than say another word about who had fears and what they were, as her remark had clearly been about Hannah. He turned to watch the race, but his attention was still on what she'd said.

What *was* Hannah afraid of? If he'd thought of her fears at all, it was that she didn't have enough of them. He'd just witnessed how little the fear of physical injury affected her. He knew she'd been hurt emotionally, but it didn't seem to curb her outgoing nature, her open interest in other people, or her willingness to risk her feelings in a personal relationship. She hadn't said she loved him in so many words, but it was there, and she wasn't shying away from it. What was she afraid of? Even absolute and total isolation hadn't frightened her, he thought, recalling an incident from several nights before.

It was long after most of the men had gone for the day, leaving a skeleton crew in the shop at the McKinnon farm. He and Trevor had hung around to make sure there weren't going to be any problems with the new transmission they were installing, the old one having sprung a leak during the trial run. Hannah had come down after dinner to fiddle for a while with the camera she'd attached to the inside of the car, making everyone laugh as she made Trevor get in and out and in and out of the car for adjustments.

"These pictures better be worth breaking my back for, Hannah," Trevor had complained, crawling out of the car for perhaps the sixth time in an hour.

"They will be. And we can use them to plaster your beautiful face over every racing magazine in the world. You'll like that, won't you?"

"It's what he lives for," Willie had muttered, sending him a simpering smile.

"All you have to do is keep the car steady and don't let it vibrate too much," Hannah had told him with a straight face, knowing she'd been asking the impossible and having already compensated for it with film and shutter speed—hopefully.

"Oh, is that all? No sweat." He'd rolled his eyes at the crew, and they'd all had a good chuckle.

When everyone had been satisfied with their efforts, the crew had left, and the four of them had started back toward the farmhouse, leaving Frank to close shop. Halfway back Hannah had suddenly remembered that she'd forgotten something— something to do with the film. She'd told them to go on without her, that she'd go back alone and catch up with them in a few minutes.

The path between the house and the shop had been pretty well lit, and it hadn't been all that great a distance, but when Hannah hadn't returned after what seemed like an awfully long time, Colt had gone back to look for her.

She hadn't heard him open the garage door, and she hadn't seen it because her back was to it, but he'd seen her. The lot lighting had been bright enough to cast light on her small form as she sat on the floor with her arms around her knees. Scared witless, he'd flicked on the overhead lights in the shop and rushed toward her.

"Hannah." She'd turned, though she hadn't heard him.

"Well, there you are," she'd said, getting to her feet and smiling. "It took you long enough. I was beginning to think that you might never miss me."

"What happened? Did you fall?" he had asked, far more disturbed than she was.

She had laughed at him. "I didn't hear Frank closing up. I was on the other side of the car picking up some film I'd dropped, and then the lights went out. I yelled at him, but I guess he didn't hear me."

"Well, what were you doing on the floor? Are you all right?"

"I'm fine," she had said, patting his cheek reassuringly. "I worked my way around the car, but when I started across to the light switches, and I couldn't feel the car anymore, it . . . well, I couldn't tell which end was up."

He had frowned, not understanding.

"I couldn't see anything," she explained as she might to a very young and inexperienced person. "And when you can't see anything, and you can't hear your footsteps or any other noise to help guide you, you can't tell if you're walking on the floor or the ceiling or up a wall. It makes me dizzy." She had shrugged and flapped her arms to her side as if it was no big deal, and walked around the car again to retrieve her film. "I decided to sit down before I fell down and wait for someone to miss me, that's all. I'm fine. Really. Although I have to say, it would have been very scary if I hadn't known what worrywarts you and Willie are."

Just the thought of the absolute and complete separation from sensory input that she'd experienced had been enough to unnerve him. Yet she had made it seem like a common occurrence.

What could be worse than that? What could be worse than facing the daily rejection and frustration of deafness? What could be worse than struggling to be a success in a competitive market with a handicap? What could be worse than fighting the people you love for your own freedom? What could be worse than . . .

He glanced back at Willie and decided that he'd read too much into her comment. Hannah might have her qualms and worries, which she didn't have any trouble facing and dealing with. But fears? Real fear? Debilitating fear? No.

Nine

"I can't put him off forever, you know," Willie yelled
at the closed door of the darkroom. Hannah was
inside, and the red light over the door was on. It
was her sanctuary. She would disappear into the
small dark room for hours at a time, knowing that
no one—not even Willie—would enter and risk
destroying her pictures. If she was indeed developing any. "It's the chance of a lifetime, and I don't
know why you aren't jumping at it, but the least
you could do is tell the guy you're not interested
and get him off *my* back."

Hannah wasn't missing any of the conversation,
even though she wasn't hearing it. It was a replay
of what Willie had been telling her almost daily for
the past three weeks. Peter Watson was most
anxious to get a decision out of Hannah about
showing her photos at Sheila Merritt's gallery, and
she was still stalling him. Willie wanted to scream
in frustration, but little good it would do her. If she
were Hannah, she'd have had her pictures downtown to the gallery so fast it would have made
Peter's head spin. Talking, even to herself, somehow made her feel better.

"You have so much talent, I can't understand why you don't want to show it off," she went on, scowling at the red light above the door, briefly suspecting that Hannah might have skipped out the back entrance and left the light on to throw Willie off her track. "You have to come out of there eventually, Hannah. And when you do . . ."

She went silent when the red light went off. The door opened and Hannah walked out, looking surprised to see her.

"Don't play innocent with me," Willie said, arms akimbo, one foot tapping furiously.

"What?" she asked, looking guileless despite Willie's order.

"You're in big trouble now. Big, big trouble," she said, using her hands to show the immensity.

"What?" She shook her open hands imploringly, wishing Willie would get to the point.

"Peter called. He talked to Gary Sherwin, who told him that your pictures for Colt's brochure were fantastic, and that he ought to try and get you a showing somewhere, that he shouldn't let you hide your talent under a basket." She frowned at Hannah's grin. "Stop that. You knew Gary was going to love those pictures. The point is, Peter knows you've finished the project, and he knows you've run out of excuses not to give him an answer."

Both her smile and her shoulders dropped in dismay. She released a heavy, heart-weary sigh and sat down.

"I wish he'd leave me alone," she said. "I wish . . ." She wished she could put off the decision indefinitely. "I don't want to tell him no, but I can't bring myself to say yes."

"Why not? It's simple. You open your mouth and say yes. What's the problem?"

"I don't know. I want to. It's what I've worked for, what I've always dreamed of. . . . But it gives me such a horrible sick feeling in my chest." Again she sighed.

"That's nerves. You're bound to be a little nervous, but that'll pass once you see what a success you'll be. They'll love your pictures. People'll beat the doors down to get you to work for them. You'll become famous . . . rich even. There'll be whole books of your pictures. Hannah," she said, disconcerted. "What have you got to lose?"

What did she have to lose?

"What time are Colt and Trevor coming to pick us up?" Willie asked when it became apparent that Hannah wasn't in the mood to bare her soul to her or ask for her advice. It was her decision. If she wanted to talk, she knew Willie would listen.

"Seven."

"Then I'm going home to get ready," she said. The little furrow of worry between Hannah's eyes, the deep sighs, and her forlorn posture touched Willie. "You'd better get ready too. Celebrate the team's victory tonight and decide what to tell Peter in the morning."

Hannah was still nodding absently, mechanically, when Willie left the house. She tried to empty her mind, to chase away the thoughts she'd been avoiding since she'd gotten the offer from the Merritt Gallery.

What did she have to lose? Nothing, she told herself. If the show bombed, it bombed. She wouldn't go blind. Those nearest her wouldn't stop loving her. She wouldn't be any worse off than she was at that moment, and yet she felt as if she had the world to lose by showing her work publicly.

She went into the studio and picked up one of the large portfolios beside her desk. It wasn't the collection of pictures she took to business meetings or showed prospective clients. She set the folder on the table and unzipped it with trembling fingers. Inside was a familiar assemblage of photographs that were her lifeblood.

Each image was a heartbeat, a breath. She knew where and when each one had been taken, what each one meant to her. Every likeness had its own history, an existence apart from hers except for the one brief instant when she'd captured it on film. Each told a truth, but not in words or deeds. Each was a personal masterpiece, a treasure she cherished, a part of herself.

She spread the pictures out over the table and took an objective look at them. They were good. Her heart ached with pride and . . . something else. Something that cast a shadow over their beauty. Something that made her want to scoop them back into the case and hide them away.

As if some demon threatened to tear them apart, she gathered up the pictures and didn't feel easy again until they were safe and secure inside the portfolio.

There was no way she could show her pictures to Sheila Merritt, she decided, patting the case lovingly with both hands. Tomorrow she'd make a trip downtown to tell Peter to decline the offer for the showing. He'd be furious, and she'd have to think of a darn good excuse in the meantime, but her decision was made. Part of her felt like weeping. The rest of her felt as if a great weight had been lifted from her shoulders. With one more resolute pat for the portfolio, she went upstairs to change her clothes before Colt arrived.

"If you two are going to hiss and spit at each other, you can stay outside," Colt said over his shoulder to Trevor and Willie as he followed Hannah into the house several hours later. "I have some sparking of my own to do, and I don't need the two of you crossing my wires."

"Have a heart, brother," Trevor whined. "Willie hasn't got the foggiest idea of what to do with a man under a full moon. Maybe if you and Hannah showed her . . ."

"It's a three-quarter moon, you idiot," Willie broke in, looking skyward.

"You see! She hasn't got a romantic bone in her body, or she'd have kept her mouth shut and let me think that I'd fooled her into thinking it was a full moon."

"Is that the kind of woman you're used to going out with?" Willie asked, disgusted. "No wonder you're warped."

"Warped? Listen, hairhead, I'll have you know . . ."

Colt didn't wait to hear the rest of the conversation. He was sure it would be another game of volley-the-insults, and as much as it amused him at times, he still hadn't been able to figure out why the two of them seemed always to be together if they harbored such dislike for each other.

Hannah laughed at him and stretched up on tiptoe to kiss him when he posed the question to her.

"You men are so silly," she said. Colt frowned and stared at her in confusion. "No one is twisting Willie's arm to get her to go out with us, you know. You're signing better and better all the time, so she doesn't need to come along to interpret for us anymore. And whose idea was it to start celebrating after every race, whether he finishes in first place or not, so long as it's somewhere in the top ten?"

"Trevor's." A light of comprehension flickered in his eyes.

"And why don't you celebrate with the rest of the team, instead of with me and Willie?"

"And why is he always so sure that you'd feel more comfortable with Willie around to interpret for you, when all she does is fight with him?" he asked, grinning sagely.

"Now you've got it," she said, pleased with his insightfulness. "Would you like some iced tea?"

"Sure. Thanks," he said, leaning back against the sink to watch her fix it. He touched her arm. "Should we throw a couple of glasses of tea on them to cool them off?"

She laughed. "The garden hose might work better."

"Have you had time to make copies of those pictures yet?" he asked, referring to some candid family and crew shots she'd taken at various times during their hot summer days together. They were private photographs taken for fun and never meant to be part of the public relations brochure she'd been hired to work on.

"Oh, yes," she said, and giggled. "They're in a large manila envelope on the table in the studio. Go get them, and we can show Trevor. There's one in there of him kissing Willie that she *says* she hates."

He gave her a naughty frown and said, "Shame on you. You're planning to throw fuel on that fire out there and laugh while you're doing it."

"Well, if heating them up doesn't work, you can always go back to throwing tea on them to cool them off."

"Very funny," he said before turning to go fetch the pictures.

"Do you want sugar in your tea?" she called.

"Yes, please."

"Colt? Do you want sugar in your tea?"

"Yes," he shouted.

"Colt! Do you want sugar in your tea?"

He was halfway across the living room before he turned back and reentered the kitchen.

"That's not fair, you know," he said. "You can yell all over the house at me, but I have to track you down and talk to you face-to-face to answer."

"I know," she said, tweaking his very ticklish

ribs with great affection. "It's great, isn't it? Most wives would give anything for an excuse as legitimate as mine to get their husbands to do that."

His expression took on a keen look of interest. His eyebrows rose like ebony arches. "We have you and me and husband and wife in the same conversation here. Are you trying to tell me something?"

"Like what?"

"Like . . . maybe you love me?"

"Maybe," she said. She fairly glowed as she slipped away from his grasping hands and hurried back to the tea. "Will you please behave yourself and go get those pictures? My ice cubes are melting."

He walked to her side. "We'll get back to this later."

"Did you ever say whether you wanted sugar in your tea or not?" she asked, grinning.

He answered her one more time to her face, and then kissed her . . . just because.

He turned on the lights in the studio. There was no manila envelope on the table, only a large portfolio.

More curious than purposefully intrusive, he unzipped the folder and took the pictures out one by one.

There wasn't anything extraordinary about the pictures, except that they seemed . . . overfocused, too sharp to him. Some were vivid images of people, so clear and real that he thought they might suddenly take a breath or speak to him. Their expressions were distinct, genuine, and unfeigned. Some were of mechanical objects in action. Others were of animals. . . .

"Oh, Lord," he muttered aloud as he became aware of what he'd stumbled into.

It was Hannah's world. What she saw but couldn't hear. Dogs barking and horses neighing.

The fire and roar of jet engines. Men weeping. The scream of pain. Women laughing. Children whispering into one another's ears. The wail of a newborn baby. Crowds cheering. It was all there in front of him. Every picture spoke to him, each making an appropriate noise in his mind.

And then, abruptly, the room went silent. Pure, absolute, unbreakable silence. The pictures became endeavor without noise, utterance without tone, emotion without sound. It was like seeing his world from inside a soundproof bubble. The sounds were there, he knew they were, they had to be. But all he was aware of was deep, unstirring silence, nothingness. He felt solitary and isolated, more alone than he'd ever felt before in his life, and it terrified him. So much so that he nearly jumped out of his skin when he heard Hannah's voice.

"What are you doing?" she asked, walking up behind him. She saw her pictures spread out on the table before him and looked at him, saying nothing, hiding her thoughts.

"This is it, isn't it?" he said, strangely amazed at the sound of his voice. "Your world. What you see and what you hear."

Hannah looked at her pictures. Each one precious and significant. Each one a torment and yet a comfort in its familiarity. Each one so much a part of her life that she couldn't deny their purpose. She nodded.

"They're incredible," he said, lifting her gaze to his face with a single finger under her chin. "I . . ." He shook his head as words failed to describe what he was feeling. He looked back to the pictures for inspiration.

"They're so real," he said. "I . . . I can hear them, Hannah." He laughed. "I know that sounds crazy, but . . ."

"No. You're supposed to hear them. You're not deaf," she said, absolving him of blame and guilt.

Willie and Peter were the only other hearing people to have seen the photos. Colt had *heard* them and understood them, and that gratified her deeply.

He looked into her eyes, deeply, beyond the hazel green, into the faraway and timeless aspects that had first attracted him to her. It was all there. Every emotion he'd seen and felt in his moment of silence was there in her soul, blended and tempered with understanding, acceptance, and wisdom.

He felt suddenly in awe of her, of her strength and courage. His heart ached with love and admiration. Once again at a loss, he looked back at the pictures, taking in each one with a new eye. Then he suddenly laughed.

"What's this one?" he asked, reaching for a picture of a bird in flight. There were other bird pictures; chirping nestlings and squawking gulls. But this one was different. It was clearly the bird's flight that she had captured.

She smiled at the picture, hoping he could understand what she was about to say.

"I know you can't hear birds flying through the sky, but I can remember what it sounds like when a bird ruffles it feathers. I must have heard it when I was young, and for some reason it made an impression on me, because sometimes I'll look up and see a bird flying by, and for just a second or two I'll think I can hear it fluttering its wings," she said with a sad little smile. "It always seems so real."

He put his arm around her shoulders and pulled her close.

"I put that picture in there as a remembered sound," she said, resting her head on his shoulder, knowing and enjoying the true meaning of sharing for a few long moments.

"They went upstairs," Colt heard Trevor whisper

gleefully from the next room. "You see! Some people think dessert is more than a piece of pie."

"You're disgusting," Willie hissed back. "To some people, having sex *means* more than having a piece of pie."

"It means more to me too," he countered. "I like sex better than pie. Shall we take the couch or go straight to the floor?"

Colt turned and had Hannah's attention following his as he led her into the studio doorway.

"I thought I told you animals to stay outside," he said, not harshly.

"It gets lonely out there in the dark when you don't have anyone to play with," Trevor complained with a pointed look at Willie. She glared back at him.

"As long as you're here, come look at something," Colt said, ignoring his brother's shenanigans. He led them all back to the table and Hannah's treasured pictures.

Trevor oohed and aahed appropriately, but it was obvious that he wasn't *hearing* the pictures the way Colt had. And Willie, who had seen the pictures before, seemed a bit amazed that they were on public display.

"You told him?" she asked Hannah, pleased but baffled.

She shook her head.

"Told me what?" Colt asked, watching Willie's shoulders shift in dismay. He turned to Hannah. "What?"

She shrugged carelessly. "Peter and Sheila Merritt want me to show my pictures."

"Not just *show* them," Willie said, frustrated with her friend. "They want to make them a show at the Merritt Gallery. It's an honor. It's important. It's what she's always wanted, and now that she's got the chance she's . . . well, she hasn't said yes yet."

"That's great," Colt said, pleased for her. "When do they—"

"I've decided not to accept," Hannah broke in.

Willie sighed loudly, angrily. Trevor looked confused. And Colt wanted to know her reasons. "Why?"

"I don't want to."

"But why? Isn't this what all photographers want? A chance to show what they can do with a camera?"

"I suppose," she said, turning to walk into the living room, not prepared to explain herself.

Colt stopped her. "I don't understand. Why don't you want to show your pictures? They're incredible," he said, repeating the only word he could think of to describe them. "You have to do this, Hannah."

"No, I don't *have* to do it. I don't want to, and I won't," she shouted at him, the familiar tightness growing in her chest, her muscles tensing.

"Are you afraid?" he asked gently, realizing the risk she was taking. "Is that it? Are you afraid no one will understand them?"

"I don't care if people understand them or not. They're only pictures," she said, lying, throwing up barriers to protect herself from whatever it was that gripped at her insides so painfully that she wanted to scream. "It's no big deal. Who wants iced tea?"

"Hannah," Colt said, taking her by the shoulders to keep her from leaving. "Look at me."

"I don't want to talk about this anymore."

He raised her chin with his fingers until she was forced to look at him. "What are you afraid of? That they won't understand the pictures? Or that they will understand them? Failure or success, Hannah? Which frightens you more?"

In a desperate rage, she pushed his hand away from her face and broke out of his hold.

"Oh, you think you're so smart," she said, shouting in her pain and fear, hating it and wanting him to feel it too. "What do you know about fear? You experienced it once and let it shatter your life. I've lived with it every day of my life. It's my constant companion. It's with me every time I leave this house. Every time I cross a street. Every time I meet a stranger. Every time I close my eyes at night. Every time. All the time. I know fear. And I know failure. My whole life is one failure after another. But I've faced my fears and recovered from my failures and gone on. If I don't want to show my pictures, if I'm afraid to show them, then I'll live with it—just like I live with my other fears."

If Colt were a lesser man, he'd have been lying on the carpet bleeding from the wounds he'd received from the tip of her rapier tongue. He felt them, and they hurt, but at that moment her pain hurt him worse.

"I don't think it's failure you're afraid of," he said in a deceptively quiet voice that she couldn't appreciate. Trevor and Willie stood in stunned silence and marveled at it. "I'm as dumb as they come about some things, but those pictures hit me like a ton of bricks. No. You're afraid you'll be a success, and that it'll turn your whole world upside down. You're afraid that people will expect more of you than you can give. You're afraid that those are the best pictures you'll ever take, and that your success will be fleeting and short-lived."

"That's not true," she said, her voice cracking, her eyes blurring with tears. She blinked hard.

"Sure it is," he said, using what signs he knew. "As long as you hoard those pictures away from the world, you're safe, aren't you? You can't even blame this on your hearing impairment. It's just you, Hannah the Human, afraid of the future and the unknown. Wondering if you have real talent, or if those were just a few lucky shots. You're in a panic over the idea that you'll never do anything better."

He was speaking fast and harsh, and she didn't catch every word, but she caught enough to get his meaning and to feel the truth. To feel the self-doubt and the sense of inferiority and imperfection in her heart. Enough to feel the shame of her weaknesses.

"Get out of my house," she said, unable to hold back the tears any longer. "All of you get out and leave me alone." She turned her back on them and covered her face with her hands, crying freely for the loss of her dreams.

Trevor and Willie, both uncomfortable, sympathetic, and irritated with Colt for driving Hannah to tears, walked gingerly between the angry lovers and left through the back door without uttering a sound. But Colt wasn't ready to leave yet.

He took a clean white handkerchief from his pocket as he walked toward the sobbing woman who meant more to him than his own life. He swallowed his abject apologies and all the kind words he wanted to offer her, and took her gently by the shoulders, boldly invading her private agony.

"I hate you," she muttered in misery. "Go away."

If a touch could communicate love, then the tender means with which he dried her tears declared his devotion to her. His patience told of his understanding. And the severity of his expression forewarned his intent.

When she was composed enough to see him clearly, though unquestionably still resentful and incensed, he spoke again.

"I'm leaving," he said, dabbing at a stray tear he'd missed, then handing her his handkerchief. "I just wanted to make sure that your eyes were dry and seeing clearly before I left. I want you to be able to see all you've accomplished since the last time you gave your heart wings."

She closed her eyes when he placed a kiss on her forehead, and didn't open them again until she felt that he was gone. She stood in the middle of her own living room, looking at piece after piece of her own furniture, thinking of her grandmother. She felt drained and exhausted, suddenly too weak to stand. Lowering herself to the bottom step of the stairwell and leaning back against the wall, she sat without thought or feeling for a long, long time.

Slowly and unconsciously, memories flickered in her mind. The day she'd moved into her house, her mother fussing about, anxious and discouraging. A twelve-year-old Willie standing at her back door watching her and her father unload box after box of her belongings until she'd finally left the house, taken a box from the back of the truck, and carried it inside without comment or question. She remembered painting the entire interior of the house while her father remodeled the studio and rewired the light sockets to the doorbell and telephone outlet.

She'd labored over a logo, and finally painted the simple sign in the front yard. The house had soon become a home, and when she had all but used up her savings and the loan money she'd gotten from the bank, she'd gotten her first catalog account and invited her parents to dinner. In a later memory, she and her father stood in the kitchen, holding each other, sharing their grief after her mother's funeral.

Her mind took a sudden turn, leaping further back in time to the birthday she'd spent with her grandmother, to the deaf school and Gallaudet, then further back to the lonely, confused soul she'd been as a young girl.

She took in a shuddering breath, returning to the present. So much had happened in her life.

Some good, some bad. Mostly ordinary things, a few thrilling victories, some sadness. But she liked her life. There were things she would change if she could, but overall she was proud of what she'd established for herself. She had been content and happy until she'd been asked to show her pictures.

And, of course, she wanted to, but . . . well, maybe she was afraid of being a success. Failure wouldn't take anything from her life. It would spur her to do better, as it had in the past. Striving to achieve was something she was used to, part of the way she lived her life. But success had the potential of change.

She tried to calculate all the possibilities that could come about if her exhibit was a success. She got as far as the money and decided that more of it wouldn't be hard to live with, then she gave up. There was more at issue than just the money, and she was too tired to think anymore. Too disheartened to evaluate any emotion lucidly.

She pulled herself to her feet and ambled slowly to the back door to lock it and turn out the lights, still contemplating the evolution of her present life. It was amazing to think of all the changes she'd undergone. Her pace got even slower as it occurred to her that when she'd confronted her mother about going to a deaf school fifteen years earlier, she hadn't known how different her life would become.

She hadn't been afraid of the future then. She hadn't given it any thought at all. She'd only known that she was miserable in the life she had, that she needed something different, something more. She walked up the stairs telling herself that she didn't need or want anything new in her life now. She was happy with the way things were.

Would a show at the Merritt Gallery make her any happier? she mused. Maybe. A little. All right, a lot. But was it worth taking the chance that it might change what she had? Even if it did cause changes, did she have so little control over her life that she couldn't pick and choose the changes she made in it?

The last question was a toughy. It required a hot, relaxing bath in the middle of the night during a sultry Virginia summer to produce an answer.

Ten

Sheila Merritt gasped. "Darling, they're fabulous."
Breathless appeared to be the woman's natural
state. She was tall and slender with poofy red hair
and an overbite, and she made Hannah extremely
uncomfortable. But who said you had to like the
people you worked with? The woman was going to
show Hannah's pictures in her gallery, she wasn't
trying out for the position of Pal of the Year.

And she did seem pleased with Hannah's work.
She lifted picture after picture into the air, exclaimed over it, and tossed it down among the
others. Always with a hand to her breast and
always with an awestruck shake of the head.

"Of course, we'll have to get them matted and
framed," she said, turning away from Hannah to
get a better light on the photograph in her hand.
"But they're sound and fury. *Pure sound and
fury.*"

"What did she say?" Hannah whispered loudly to
Willie, who signed for her. "Sound and fury?" she
asked, watching the woman closely.

"Darling, I can actually hear this dog barking,
and I can *feel* the passion in every single one of

these pictures. They're simply fabulous," she said, speaking so quickly that Hannah had to once again turn to Willie. "We'll call the exhibit 'The Sound and Fury of Silence.' I love it." And then without looking at her, she said, "Unless, of course, you had another title in mind, dear."

Hannah didn't have any other title in mind. She was still trying to get used to the fact that she'd actually accepted Ms. Merritt's offer to show her pictures.

"'The Sound and Fury of Silence' is fine with me," she said, feeling too inexperienced to question the woman's judgment. "Let's just hope they signify more than nothing."

"What was that?" Sheila asked with one of her rare direct looks at Hannah.

"Ah . . . Shakespeare," she said, feeling awkward. "'Full of sound and fury, signifying nothing'?"

"Yes. Well, there's no need to worry about that, dear. My best friends will tell you that I am supremely insensitive for a woman, and they've touched me. Moved me. Deeply."

It was hard to gauge how deep "deeply" was in the woman, but Hannah had no recourse other than to trust that her inspiration in show titles wouldn't become another one of those misquoted truths. Like "absence makes the heart grow fonder . . . for someone new."

She also had no recourse other than to trust that Colt's absence didn't mean he'd found someone new. If she let herself think anything else, she'd go insane. It was early Thursday afternoon, and she hadn't seen or heard from him since Monday night. It seemed like forever.

People in love had arguments. Sometimes lots of arguments. It didn't necessarily mean anything bad, she kept telling herself. Arguments could be good, even healthy for a relationship, she reminded herself. So why did she feel as if she were falling apart? Why was it taking a concentrated effort to remain calm and to continue trusting that he'd show up again?

Maybe it was the calls she'd made to him through his TDD's that had gone unanswered. Maybe it was because she was feeling remorse for all the things she'd said to him. For lashing out at him unfairly, deliberately causing him pain in order to ease her own. Maybe it was because she couldn't blame him if he had changed his mind about loving her. Maybe . . .

"Do you want me to call for you?" Willie asked back at the house, managing to look irritated and sympathetic at the same time.

"Call who?"

"Who do you think? It's been three days, and he didn't have nearly as much to forgive as you did. Maybe he thinks you're still angry at him. Maybe he's waiting for you to contact him."

She gave up trying to pretend that she didn't know what Willie was talking about and shook her head. "I've already tried to contact him. He hasn't answered any of my calls."

"Maybe he's out of town."

"No race until next week," she said, falling onto the couch, depressed and sinking fast into despair. "I checked."

"Maybe he's at the farm. He hasn't had a TDD installed there yet, has he?"

She shook her head. She'd taken comfort in the fact that he hadn't had the other two disconnected.

"I'll call the farm. Mrs. McKinnon will know where he is," Willie said, and smiled. "Guys may forget to call the women they're in love with, but they never forget to call their mothers."

Hannah refused to take cheer. "I don't want to

seem pushy. If he doesn't want to talk to me, I . . ."

Willie growled her frustration, rolled her eyes, and stood to walk to the phone.

Hannah watched, her heart pumping hard and fast with anxiety as Willie dialed a number, wrote something on a pad of paper, hung up, and dialed again. When her lips began to move, Hannah developed tunnel vision to catch her words.

She exchanged pleasantries, then she asked if Mrs. McKinnon had seen Colt lately. She grinned at Hannah and nodded an I-told-you-so. When she asked to speak with him, Hannah stood and moved to her side. She was about to chicken out and tell Willie not to speak to him. Her pride wanted to say that knowing he was all right and at the farm was enough, and that he'd call when he was ready. But then she noticed Willie's frown, and that the pale skin under her freckles had suddenly turned ashen. She felt a sickness in her chest.

"Has something happened to Trevor?" Willie asked.

Hannah saw the tension drain from her body, but the look she received still had a great deal of concern and apprehension in it. She nodded several times and finally said good-bye.

"What?" Hannah asked the question before the receiver hit its cradle. "What's wrong? Is Colt okay?"

"Yes. But we have to go now," she said, flustered in an un-Willie-like way. "Where are your keys?"

"Why? What's happened?"

"Where's your purse?" she asked, her back to Hannah.

"Willie! What's happening?"

She turned and took a deep breath. "I caught Mrs. McKinnon on her way to Martinsville. Trevor and the whole crew are there today," she said, pausing to find words to continue, coming up with only two. "Colt's driving."

The two-hour drive between Richmond and Roanoke took forever, even with Willie driving. Where Willie compared Hannah's driving to that of someone's grandmother, Hannah said Willie's was more like a bat out of hell. Yet every minute seemed like an hour and every mile seemed like a hundred.

Neither spoke. Willie was worried about Hannah . . . and Colt . . . and Trevor, all for different reasons but in equal measures. What if something happened to Colt? What if he'd decided to drive the car with the best of intentions and with a clear mind, but suddenly lost them at two hundred miles an hour? What if the fury and fear that she'd witnessed at the farm paralyzed him? What if he couldn't control the car? What if . . . What would Trevor do? What would happen to Hannah? She pressed a little harder on the gas pedal.

Hannah kept her eyes fixed on the road, her mind speeding miles ahead of the car. It was all her fault. She'd belittled his fear and his pain, and now he felt he had to prove himself. She was such a fool. How could she hurt the best thing that had ever happened in her life? How could she have been so cruel? Didn't he know that he didn't have to prove anything to her? Didn't he know how wonderful he was? What if something happened to him? She was such a fool. First her mother, and now Colt. She always hurt those who meant the most to her. Didn't he know how important he was to her? Why hadn't she told him? Why hadn't she told him that she loved him?

The road from Roanoke to Martinsville was interminable. Hannah sat forward, as if doing so would get her there sooner. Just beyond the fenced main gate they caught sight of the bumblebee-yellow car being towed by the familiar blue van, followed by several trucks, cars, and a rescue vehicle leaving the grounds. They were too late.

Most of the caravan came to a stop on the track side of the main gate as the two women approached it, the emergency transport driving on in no great hurry. They couldn't see the driver of the van as yet, but he had apparently recognized their car.

Hannah's attention was drawn to the race car behind the van. It was whole and undamaged. Whereas some chemical changes were loud and obvious, the conversion that began to take place within her was subtle and indistinct. It registered in her mind that the car's condition was an indication that Colt was all right, but it didn't decrease the overwhelming turmoil she felt. In fact, the agitation increased.

When Colt stepped from the driver's side of the car and Willie came to a stop a yard or so away from him, Hannah knew she should have been overpowered with relief and gratitude, but she wasn't.

When she saw that he was grinning triumphantly, she felt a peculiar urge to break something, an urge that was curiously inconsistent with the joy she knew she should have been feeling.

She began to tremble from within, like a simmering volcano. The transformation of the emotional elements inside of her had completed itself. A quiet riot exploded in her mind, and her body felt supercharged with adrenaline. She was crazed with anger as she all but ripped the car door from its hinges and got out.

Colt looked smug and excited to see her as he approached with his arms stretched out in loving welcome.

"Hi," she saw him say. He laughed. "You're a miracle. I was just wishing you were here, and here you are. I've—" Hannah slugged his arm as

hard as she could . . . and felt a whole lot better.
"Ow! What was that for?" he asked, stepping away
from a second punch, floored and confused.

"Did you drive that thing?" she asked, pointing
to the car, her voice high-pitched and strained
with emotions she'd never known before. "Did you
drive it?"

"Yes."

She stepped forward and took another poorly
aimed swing at him. "You are so stupid!" she cried,
unconscious of the tears that rolled down her
cheeks. "You're the dumbest man I've ever met,
and I'm beginning to wish I hadn't. How could
you?"

"What?" he asked, more bewildered. He took her
hands into his for his own safety, and approached
with caution. "What?"

"Don't touch me," she said, struggling to get
free, all too aware of the heat of his hands at her
wrists and how purely glad she was that he'd come
to no harm. Glad, but still mad. "I don't want you
to touch me. You're a stupid, stupid man, and I
don't want you ever to touch me again. I can't
believe you'd do such a thing."

"What?!" He gave her a firm shake, aware that
Willie, his mother and brother, and the rest of the
crew were watching. He simply didn't know what
else to do.

She went stock-still in his grasp and looked at
him. "I know why you did it, Colt. It was my fault,
and I'm sorry, but it was a stupid thing for you to
do."

He shook his head, still unable to comprehend
what he'd done to create such fury in her. He was
already sorry for whatever it was, but he needed a
specific crime in order to apologize.

"What did I do, Hannah?"

"You drove that stupid car because of what I said
the other night. I shouldn't have said what I did,

and I didn't really mean it, I . . . I just wanted to hurt you. I wanted you to go away and leave me alone. And I'm sorry for that. I don't ever want you to go away again. But I never dreamed you would do something like this," she said, her words gradually softening as the energy she'd used to free herself from her fears and sustain her anger slowly ebbed away.

"You're mad that I drove the car?" he asked, wanting to be sure of her complaint.

"I'm mad that I made you feel as if you had to prove yourself by driving it, yes." With her hands still firmly caught in his, she had to bend her head to wipe away tears from her chin and cheeks. "It was a stupid thing to do. You don't have to prove yourself to anyone, Colt. Least of all me. I already love you."

Colt's expression softened as he released the huge, anxious breath he'd been holding in his lungs. He wanted to holler with joy. She loved him! She'd been worried about him. She cared. But it just didn't seem like the right moment.

When she sniffed and lowered her head again to rub her nose on her fingers, he caught Trevor's eye and motioned him to evacuate the grounds. He held her hands in one of his and retrieved a handkerchief for her with the other. He tucked it between her fingers and, still holding her wrists, watched with great tenderness as she wiped her eyes and nose.

The motion of the vehicles leaving attracted her attention, and she looked up.

"Where are they going?" she asked, taking note that Willie had left with the others.

"Back to the farm," he said, watching her as if he couldn't believe she was real. "We'll drive your car back later."

"Later? After what?" She took a final dab at her nose.

"After you and I have a little talk." He led her the two or three feet to her car and leaned up against it to get comfortable.

"About what?" Dread settled into her heart.

"About you and me and what I did today."

Hannah knew what was coming. He couldn't forgive her. She'd hurt him too badly. He'd overcome his fear, and was going back to driving race cars. There wouldn't be room in his life for her anymore.

"First of all," he said when she finally looked at him. "What you said the other night didn't have anything to do with what happened here today. Trevor and I planned this in the car on our way over to pick you and Willie up for dinner that night. I was going to invite you to come and watch, but . . . well, then the chance just didn't present itself."

"I don't understand," she said, finding that even though he still had ahold of her wrists, he was no longer impeding her movements. "Why? Why did you want to drive all of sudden?" She felt weak at the thought of what could have happened to him. She reached out and touched his cheek and murmured his name. "If anything had happened to you . . ." she said, unable to finish the sentence as she shook the possibilities from her mind.

He smiled at her concern, and was eager to get back to her declaration of love, but he knew this had to be settled first.

"It was time, Hannah." It was hard for him to explain. "I don't know. . . . It just seemed like the right time. Like it was time to bury the past and let go of my guilt and pain and go on with my life." He played with several wayward curls near her face as he continued. "That day you drove the race car . . . It was everything I told you about, but it was more than that too. This was the only place in the world where I couldn't follow you or be there for you if you needed me, or even just be with you. The whole time you were gone that day, it ate at me. And then to find out that you'd put yourself in that kind of danger . . . and that Trevor had *let* you . . . I don't know. It made me crazy."

"But I was very careful, and I didn't go very fast," she said. "My eyes couldn't keep up with the speed of everything flashing past. It was like a sensory overload. I only went around three or four times before I had to stop." She laughed lightly. "And then I stopped on the far side of the track and got out dizzy, so Trevor had to bring it the rest of the way around. He was silly all the way back to the farm, trying to make me feel better."

"I know," he said. "He told me all about it later. But that wasn't the whole thing. It was more. It was you here and me back at the farm. I know I can't stop you from doing what you want to do, but it's important for me to think that I'm there for you if you ever need me. I couldn't have stopped you from driving the car, but if you'd needed me, I wouldn't have been there either. Can you under-stand that?"

"Yes. I think so," she said, more sure of the warm feelings his words evoked in her heart.

"But even that wasn't all of it," he said, still having difficulty finding words. He pushed himself away from the car and stepped around her. He was too close to her to think straight. He walked several feet away, then turned back to her and continued to speak. "It was later that night, after we'd talked and I'd told you all about Joey and everything. It just didn't seem important anymore. It was," he amended quickly, "but it wasn't. That doesn't make sense."

"Yes, it does," she said, following in his steps to be close to him—not ever wanting to be too far from him again. "People grieve in lots of different ways. When my mother died, I grieved by going out of my way to do everything that frightened me the most, just to keep showing her that I could. You grieved for your friend by giving up what you both loved the most, what he couldn't do anymore. And I hate to sound trite, but time does heal all wounds. You simply discovered that you'd punished yourself enough, and that time had allowed your wounds to heal."

Again, as he had so many times before, he looked deep into her eyes. Her eyes that seemed to see from some faraway place and distant time that was filled with things he shouldn't or couldn't possibly know about. He wanted to tell her how creepy it was, how he sometimes imagined there was an ancient sorceress or some wise and all-knowing power within her. But it was also what made her special to him, what had attracted and continued to attract him to her.

"You're a little spooky sometimes, you know that?" he asked, his hands on her shoulders.

"What was that?"

He finger-spelled "spooky" for her.

"Like a ghost?" she asked.

He shook his head. "Like some wonderfully magical thing that can't be explained. You keep me wondering and on the edge of my chair most of the time."

"Good," she said, and grinned. "Willie tells me it's good to keep a man guessing."

He feigned shock and dismay. "Don't tell me you're taking lessons from that knothead. She sounds like Trevor."

"I have my own way of doing things," she said, smiling coyly.

He smiled, too, but not coyly.

"That's true enough." He rubbed the arm she'd

hit earlier. "You have a real unique way of getting a man's attention."

"I was mad."

"I noticed." He laughed. "Do you know that you told me that you loved me?"

"I was mad, not insane. Of course I remember."

He gave her a patient stare. When she didn't respond, he lifted his eyebrows and asked, "Well? Aren't you going to tell me again? Now that you're not mad anymore?"

"Maybe." She tried to step away, but his hands held her firmly.

"Tell me."

"You're such a pushy guy," she said playfully.

"Tell me."

"It's not easy to love a deaf woman, you know."

"You're tellin' me," he said, muttering intentionally.

"What was that?" she asked suspiciously, digging her fingers into his ribs and watching him squirm. "What did you just say?"

"I said, 'it isn't easy to love any woman . . . except you.'"

"That's not what you said," she said, tickling his ribs unmercifully. "Tell me the truth."

He shied away from her, laughing, and took a new approach to getting what he wanted. He overpowered her. Grabbing both her hands and holding them tightly behind her, he lowered his face to hers, covering her mouth with his.

He kissed her long, hard, and deeply. When she returned his passion and pressed her breasts tightly against his chest in an effort to get closer, he moaned his pleasure. When she plunged her tongue into his mouth, teasing and enticing, he forgot that she was his prisoner, and released her hands to pull her closer and tighter to him.

She wound her arms around his neck and clung to him as he carried her to that place into which the waters flow and the winds blow, the final destination of all that is clean and pure and everlasting. There she found their love.

"I've been patient long enough," he said when she opened her eyes to look at him. "Tell me, Hannah."

"I love you."

Eleven

There was a quiet family celebration at the McKinnon farm that night. Mrs. McKinnon set the table with enough food to feed a small army. And the five of them laughed and teased good-naturedly until the last pot was washed and put away.

Colt made a major production of opening a bottle of his mother's sweet apple wine to toast Hannah's opening.

"Here's to 'The Sound and Fury of Silence,'" he said when everyone had their glasses held high. He rubbed the small bruise on his arm and grinned. "May the impact it has on the rest of the world be as awakening as it was for me. Here's to Hannah's beautiful eyes, her camera, and all the success she can tolerate."

"Hear, hear . . . so to speak," Trevor said, taking a sip of his wine as he stood to make his own toast. "Here's to women everywhere."

Willie made a sputtering noise and glared at him.

"You're depraved," she said, refusing to drink to his salute.

"Did you hear that, Mama?" he asked, attempting to look insulted. "Is liking women depraved?"

"The way you like them?" his mother asked thoughtfully. "Yes, dear, I think it is."

"Sit down, showboat," Willie said, grinning at Mrs. McKinnon. "It's my turn."

She stood and held up her glass. "Here's to Hannah. To her dedication, her hard work, and the love she gives so freely. Thanks for being my friend, Hannah."

Hannah sat beside Colt on the couch feeling extremely self-conscious and humble. She owed these people so much more than she'd ever given them. Yet here they were toasting her as if she were someone special. She felt she ought to say something, but Mrs. McKinnon spoke first.

She remained seated in her rocking chair, but held out her glass. "Here's to Hannah and her show. May it be a great success, and may she have many more—I love a good excuse to go to Richmond. Here's to Willie, an astute young woman, whose assistance to Hannah has been invaluable, I'm sure."

"Invaluable," Hannah agreed.

"But whose true talent lies in being able to call a spade a spade," she added, winking at Willie.

"What's this?" Trevor asked, sitting up as if someone had pinched him. "Oh, Mama. Give me a break. There'll be no living with her now."

Willie cast him a saccharin-sweet smile when his mother ignored him and went on.

"And here's to my sons. Two men no mother could be prouder of, who have brought me great joy, and who I'm sure will remember to spray my apple trees before they leave tomorrow, so the bugs won't get 'em."

"Spoken like a true mother." Colt and Trevor groaned playfully at the same time. "Stop. You're breaking my heart."

They all laughed, and in the end Hannah never found an opportunity to make a toast of her own.

She wasn't sure what she would have said. Something corny no doubt. Something that didn't come near to expressing the way she felt inside. How could one put into words the deep gratitude one felt for the unconditional love and acceptance they had bestowed upon her? She sighed her contentment and decided it was just as well that she didn't have to try.

The night wore on in much the same manner. A Monopoly board was brought out during a challenge between Trevor and Willie. Colt and Hannah agreed to play if no blood was shed. And Mrs. McKinnon became the impartial banker until well after midnight, when she decided to retire.

"We didn't discuss it before, but I hope you girls aren't planning to drive home tonight," she said, stiffly pushing herself out of the rocking chair. "I made up the two rooms you used last time, and you know you're certainly welcome to use them."

"Thank you, Mrs. McKinnon," Hannah said.

"Call me Ruth, dear. When people call me Mrs. McKinnon, it reminds me of my mother-in-law—a horrible woman who's been dead for twenty-two years."

Willie giggled. Ruth McKinnon was a woman after her own heart. She waited until the older woman was out of hearing range, then she commented, "Poor thing. She could have saved herself a lot of trouble making up that second bed if she knew that only three beds were used the last time we stayed here." She giggled again and watched her friend's cheeks turn pink. "Hannah got into the bed with her clothes on the next morning to make it *look* as if she'd slept there."

Hannah cringed inwardly. She wasn't ashamed that she'd spent the night with Colt, and she wasn't proud of deceiving his mother. She just wasn't sure how Mrs. McKinnon felt about premarital sex, and long habit demanded that she at least

attempt to present a positive image of herself—
though, Lord knew, she'd probably made enough
noise to wake Mrs. McKinnon's dead mother-in-
law that night anyway. The whole incident was
very embarrassing and not what she cared to
discuss over a game of Monopoly.

"You behave, Willie Willis," she said in a threatening manner. She wagged her eyebrows in a
dramatic display of wickedness, and added, "Or I'll
tell Trevor your real name."

Trevor jumped on her threat like a fly on doo-
doo.

"She has a real name! I knew it," he said gleefully. "No one could name their kid Willie Willis on
purpose. I knew you had to have a real name. What
is it?"

When Willie refused to answer and Hannah merely
shook her head like a keeper of great secrets, he
started guessing.

"It's Wilhelmina."

"No."

"Wilma."

"No."

"Willonda."

"That's Yolanda, idiot. And no, that's not my
name. See the can of worms you've opened?" she
said to Hannah, not really angry. "I won't know a
moment's peace with this moron now."

"Wilfred."

"Will you stop? I wouldn't tell you my real name if
you tied me to the back of a herd of wild horses."

"Wilma."

"You already guessed that one. Who's turn is it,
anyway?" she asked, turning back to the board
game.

The games—Monopoly and Name That Willie—
continued until after one-thirty, when Colt began
to yawn loud and long, broadly hinting that it was
time to go to bed. If it had been up to him, he'd

have skipped dinner and the sweet apple wine and the after-dinner games and conversation, and taken Hannah straight to his bed when they'd returned from the track at dusk. He was feeling virtuous in the extreme that he'd shared her with the others at all. But enough was enough.

Every time she leaned forward to throw the dice and take her turn, his head would fill with the sweet scent of her. Every time she adjusted her position on the couch beside him or their thighs rubbed, his muscles tensed and anticipation churned low and deep in his gut. Every time he glanced at her face—watchful, laughing, or deep in concentration—he would find himself staring at her and experiencing a profound yearning to touch her. Yes, indeed. Enough was enough.

"Well, I don't know about the rest of you, but tomorrow's a workday for me," he said, stretching his overtaxed muscles and stifling another yawn. "I'm going to bed."

Trevor leaned close to Willie's ear and without lowering his voice said, "Are you wondering whose bed he's going to?"

"Telling secrets isn't permitted in my presence, you know," Hannah said in genial innocence. "They make me paranoid."

"Ignore me, Hannah," Trevor said. "I'm jealous. I've been trying to coax Willie into bed for weeks now, and she won't have anything to do with me."

Willie lowered her head and let her hair hide her expression. But for just an instant, Hannah thought she saw her smile.

"She's smart," Colt said.

"So am I," Hannah said, slipping her hand into Colt's. "And I think I'll follow you up to bed."

Trevor fell on the floor, groaning in agony.

"Colt. I'm your baby brother. Help me." He moaned. "Tell me your secret."

"What's he doing?" Hannah asked, unable to see

what he was saying. She grinned at Willie's signs.

Colt smiled with superiority. He turned his back on his poor starving brother and led Hannah to the stairs with a certain display of studliness. He started her up the steps in front of him, patted her lovingly on the bottom, and then turned to look at Trevor.

"Try honey, brother," he said, his tone lofty. "It's sweeter than vinegar."

Hannah turned out the bathroom light feeling cool and refreshed from her shower. Colt was stretched out in bed, reading while he waited for her. Catching him in a quiet moment of repose was something unusual. She took the moment just to look at him and to feel incredibly lucky that he'd walked into her life.

"How come my T-shirts look better on you than they do on me?" he asked when he glanced over and found her watching him. He dropped the book he was reading to the floor and curled his index finger at her, beckoning her to come to him.

"Maybe because I make them bulge in different places," she said, walking to the bed and climbing up to straddle him.

"That must be it. You have much better bulges than I do." He drew both hands down the front of the shirt, and she instinctively bowed her back to press her sensitive breasts into the palms of his hands. Then his hands settled at her hips, his thumbs rubbing lazily against her inner thighs. He took a deep breath, saying, "You even make my soap smell better."

"We need to talk," she said, removing his hands from a place where he knew she was vulnerable, and stacking them on his chest.

"You look so serious."

"It's a serious subject."

"Okay. What is it?"

"Will you be going back to driving in the races now?"

"I've been waiting for this," he said, unfolding his hands to place them back on her hips. He sighed and looked at her thoughtfully. "How would you feel about it if I did?"

"Truth?"

"Of course."

"I don't want you to do it. I know how much it means to you, and I know I can't stop you, but I don't want you to."

"Why?"

"Why?" She thought it a stupid question. "Because I love you, and it's dangerous. I don't want anything to happen to you."

He nodded, lowering his gaze from hers. "If I went back to driving, you'd know how it feels to worry the way I do when you insist on doing things that aren't safe." He looked at her then. "But no, I'm not planning on it. I'm out of condition, and I've lost my edge. And to tell you the truth, I really do enjoy what I'm doing now, putting the whole thing together and making it run." He held up a cautioning finger. "But that's not saying I won't ever drive laps just for fun. It is fun, Hannah, and I've missed it all these years."

"But you'll be careful." It was more a question than a statement.

"Are you kidding me? With everything in the world to live for, don't you think I'd be careful?"

She set her elbows down on his chest, her chin in her fists, and then grinned mischievously. "That's me, right? Everything in the world to live for?"

The T-shirt began to slide up her hips and past her ribs as he said, "You are my world, Hannah."

Breakfast at Ruth McKinnon's table looked like a church smorgasbord. Hannah sat down in dismay, without the slightest idea of what to eat first.

Colt entered the room behind her a short while later, fresh from his shower. He put his hands on her shoulders and a kiss on her cheek before crossing the kitchen to steal a piece of the bacon his mother was cooking.

"Mornin', Mama," he said, hugging her from behind as she stood in her favorite place over the stove. He kissed her cheek as well. "Sorry I'm late. I was mussing my sheets so you wouldn't know where I slept last night."

"Heaven help me, Colt," she said, swatting his hand with her spatula when he reached for a second piece of bacon. "You and Hannah are going to drive me to an early grave if I have to keep making up clean beds. Have mercy on me and marry the girl, will you?"

"I will. All in good time, Mama," he said, grinning.

"Mama. Colt. Good morning," Trevor said cheerfully as he entered the room. He brushed Hannah's back as he walked past her and smiled his greeting to her when she looked up. "When was the last time you saw a day as beautiful as this one?"

Hannah watched as Colt and his mother turned to stare at Trevor as if he'd just announced the end of the world. Then they exchanged knowing glances.

Colt brought two cups of coffee to the table and offered one to Hannah before he sat down beside her.

"Good morning, everyone," Willie said as she breezed into the kitchen. "Mrs. McKinnon, this looks great. I'm starving."

"Ruth, dear," she said mildly. "And you dig right in. We'll put some meat on those bones of yours yet."

While Willie poured her own coffee, Colt squeezed Hannah's knee under the table and motioned with his head for her to take a look at Trevor. He had come to attention beside Willie's chair and was watching her intently. When she walked back to the table, he exhibited the definition of savoir faire.

"Please. Allow me," he said, holding her chair out for her.

"Why, thank you," she said, bestowing upon him her most gracious smile. "Beautiful morning, isn't it?"

They grinned at each other, exchanging secrets with their eyes.

"Would you care for some pancakes?"

"Ah, no. Thank you. I believe I'll start with the eggs."

Colt and Hannah traded glances and astute thoughts.

"Toast?"

"You're so kind."

Ruth McKinnon, following the sticky-sweet conversation at the other end of the table, sat down across from Hannah, rolling her eyes. Hannah stuck her index finger in her mouth and made a terrible face as if she were trying to gag herself, and Ruth laughed. Colt lowered his gaze to his plate and continued to eat.

"Would you care for some of my mother's home-made apple jelly or apple butter on your toast?" Trevor asked. "Or perhaps some . . . honey?"

Willie giggled. "Some more honey would be nice, thank you."

Colt mouthed the word "more" for Hannah and his mother, and they smirked.

"Please allow me." He took the honey stick from the pot and dappled it on Willie's toast, and then with the stick poised, he asked, "May I?"

"I wish you would."

Ever so carefully he touched her upper and lower

lips with the stick, then very deliberately leaned forward to suck the honey from her mouth.

They cheered and clapped at the other end of the table.

"Well, it's about time," Ruth said, well satisfied. "And I suppose I have another clean bed to make up now too."

Hannah blushed, and Ruth winked at her.

"Two beds ought to be plenty from now on, Mama," Trevor said, grinning at Willie, who didn't bother to blush. She had what she'd set out to catch, and she didn't care who knew it.

"And if you get too full of yourself again, you can sleep in the shop with the cars," Willie said, teasing him.

"Full of myself? Me?" He looked shocked. "Isn't that just like a woman?" He looked from Hannah to his mother, then to his brother. "You show a little self-confidence, and they shoot you down every time."

"A little self-confidence?" It was Willie's turn to act shocked. "Trevor, your head is so big, I'm surprised it isn't black and blue from pushing it through doors."

"Oh, yeah? Well, I've been thinking the same thing about your hair. If you used hair spray, we'd have to put in double-wide doors just to have you over for dinner."

"I thought you liked my hair."

He leaned sideways to kiss her again. "I said I was getting attached to it—which could have meant that I had my arm stuck in it." He paused. "But lucky for you, I meant it as a compliment. It's as endearing to me as you are, my Sweet Harmony."

"What was that?" Hannah asked rudely. Words between lovers were usually best left untouched, but she couldn't believe what her eyes had just seen. "What did he say?" she asked Colt. "What did you just call her?" she asked Trevor.

Trevor grinned, and Willie mumbled, "Now you've done it."

"He called her his sweet harmony," Colt said, looking nauseous. "And if he does it again, I'm going to throw cold water on him."

"You told him?" Hannah said. She slouched back in her chair, her eyes wide and her mouth open in utter astonishment.

"It slipped out. I wasn't thinking straight."

"What did she tell him?" Colt asked, looking confused, as was his mother.

"Her real name."

"Her name?" Mother and son replayed the last part of the conversation over in their heads and frowned at each other at the same time. They looked at Willie and then turned to Hannah for the truth.

"Her name's Sweet Harmony?"

She nodded. "Sweet Harmony Willis."

Trevor burst into peals of laughter as his mother and brother slowly turned their heads to stare at Willie in profound disbelief.

She shrugged and shook her head, lamenting her mother's foul deed. Finally she said, "My mother calls herself a political activist now, but when I was born, she was just a plain ol' flower-totin' hippie."

Author's Note

My research for this book was the most interesting and insightful work I've ever done. I highly recommend you read *Life as a Spectator Sport* by Cheryl Heppner, to be published by Gallaudet University Press, 800 Florida Avenue N.E., Washington D.C. 20002, in June of 1992. It's not a romance, but it is a story about loving life and the determination it takes to participate in it.

THE EDITOR'S CORNER

With the six marvelous **LOVESWEPT**s coming your way next month, it certainly will be the season to be jolly. Reading the best romances from the finest authors—what better way to enter into the holiday spirit?

Leading our fabulous lineup is the ever-popular Fayrene Preston with **SATAN'S ANGEL**, LOVESWEPT #510. Nicholas Santini awakes after a car crash and thinks he's died and gone to heaven—why else would a beautiful angel be at his side? But Angel Smith is a flesh-and-blood woman who makes him burn with a desire that lets him know he's very much alive. Angel's determined to work a miracle on this magnificent man, to drive away the pain—and the peril—that torments him. A truly wonderful story, written with sizzling sensuality and poignant emotions—one of Fayrene's best!

How appropriate that Gail Douglas's newest LOVESWEPT is titled **AFTER HOURS,** #511, for that's when things heat up between Casey McIntyre and Alex McLean. Alex puts his business—and heart—on the line when he works *very* closely with Casey to save his newspaper. He's been betrayed before, but Casey inspires trust . . . and brings him to a fever pitch of sensual excitement. She never takes orders from anyone, yet she can't seem to deny Alex's passionate demands. A terrific book, from start to finish.

Sandra Chastain weaves her magical touch in **THE-JUDGE AND THE GYPSY,** LOVESWEPT #512. When Judge Rasch Webber unknowingly shatters her father's dream, Savannah Ramey vows a Gypsy's revenge: She would tantalize him beyond reason, awakening longings he's denied, then steal what he most loves. She couldn't know she'd be entangled in a web of desire, drawn to the velvet caress of Rasch's voice and the ecstatic fulfillment in his arms. You'll be thoroughly enchanted with this story of forbidden love.

The combination of love and laughter makes **MIDNIGHT KISS** by Marcia Evanick, LOVESWEPT #513, completely irresistible. To Autumn O'Neil, Thane Clayborne is a sexy stick-in-the-mud, and she delights in making him lose control. True, running a little wild is not Thane's style, but Autumn's seductive beauty tempts him to let go. Still, she's afraid that the man who bravely sacrificed a dream for another's happiness could never care for a woman who ran scared when it counted most. Another winner from Marcia Evanick!

With his tight jeans, biker boots, and heartbreak-blue eyes, Michael Hayward is a **TEMPTATION FROM THE PAST**, LOVESWEPT #514, by Cindy Gerard. January Stewart has never seen a sexier man, but she knows he's more trouble that she can handle. Intrigued by the dedicated lawyer, Michael wants to thaw January's cool demeanor and light her fire. Is he the one who would break down her defenses and cast away her secret pain? Your heart will be stirred by this touching story.

A fitting final course is **JUST DESSERTS** by Theresa Gladden, LOVESWEPT #515. Caitlin MacKenzie has had it with being teased by her new housemate, Drew Daniels, and she retaliates with a cream pie in his face! Pleased that serious Caitie has a sense of humor to match her lovely self, Drew begins an ardent pursuit. She would fit so perfectly in the future he's mapped out, but Catie has dreams of her own, dreams that could cost her what she has grown to treasure. A sweet and sexy romance—what more could anybody want?

FANFARE presents four truly spectacular books this month! Don't miss bestselling Amanda Quick's **RENDEZ-VOUS.** From London's most exclusive club to an imposing country manor, comes this provocative tale about a free-thinking beauty, a reckless charmer, and a love that defied all logic. **MIRACLE,** by beloved LOVESWEPT author Deborah Smith, is the unforgettable contemporary romance of passion and the collision of worlds, where a man and a woman who couldn't have been more different learn that love may be improbable, but never impossible.

Immensely talented Rosalind Laker delivers the exquisite historical **CIRCLE OF PEARLS.** In England during the days of plague and fire, Julia Pallister's greatest test comes from an unexpected quarter—the man she calls enemy, a man who will stop at nothing to win her heart. And in **FOREVER,** by critically acclaimed Theresa Weir, we witness the true power of love. Sammy Thoreau had been pronounced a lost cause, but from the moment Dr. Rachel Collins lays eyes on him, she knows she would do anything to help the bad-boy journalist learn to live again.

Happy reading!

With every good wish for a holiday filled with the best things in life,

Nita Taublib

Nita Taublib
Associate Publisher/LOVESWEPT
Publishing Associate/FANFARE

FANFARE

Now On Sale

MIRACLE
(29107-6) $4.50/5.50 in Canada
by Deborah Smith
author of THE BELOVED WOMAN

A man and a woman who couldn't have been more different -- all it took to bring them together was a MIRACLE. "Ever witty, a sparkling talent with a unique voice." -- Rendezvous

CIRCLE OF PEARLS
(29423-7) $5.99/6.99 in Canada
by Rosalind Laker
author of TO DANCE WITH KINGS

Why is Julia Pallister so drawn to the man she is sure she despises, the enemy her Royalist stepfather would have her marry? "A book to sit back and enjoy like a sumptuous feast." -- Rave Reviews

FOREVER
(29380-X) $4.50/5.50 in Canada
by Theresa Weir
author of AMAZON LILY

They said he was a lost cause, but they didn't know what love could do. "[A] hauntingly beautiful and passionate love story." -- Rendezvous

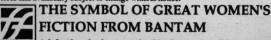

FANFARE

On Sale in November

THE FLAMES OF VENGEANCE

(29375-3) $4.99/5.99 in Canada

by Beverly Byrne

bestselling author of A LASTING FIRE and
THE MORGAN WOMEN

*There are fires fed by passion and fires fed by greed . . . most terrible of all
are the fires set ablaze by cruelty and injustice. But can love, tenderness,
and honor survive the fire storm created by the need to destroy?*

REDEEMING LOVE

(29368-0) $3.99/4.99 in Canada

by Francine Rivers

author of A REBEL IN HIS ARMS

*Sold into prostitution as an orphan, beautiful and tormented Angel never
believed in love. But when Michael Hosea pursues her, showering her
with unconditional love, he opens Angel's eyes to life's sweetest blessings.*

22 INDIGO PLACE

(29085-1) $4.50/5.50 in Canada

by Sandra Brown

<u>New York Times</u> bestselling author of
TEXAS! LUCKY and TEXAS! CHASE

*To James, Laura had always been the girl he couldn't have, the rich man's
daughter for whom he had never been good enough. But on a moonlit
night, his fervent kiss binds her to him forever.*

"Funny and heartrending . . . wonderful characters . . . I laughed out loud and couldn't stop reading. A splendid romance!" -- *Susan Elizabeth Phillips, New York Times bestselling author of FANCY PANTS and HOT SHOT*

Miracle

by

Deborah Smith

An unforgettable story of love and the collision of two worlds. From a shanty in the Georgia hills to a television studio in L.A., from the heat and dust of Africa to glittering Paris nights -- with warm, humorous, passionate characters, MIRACLE weaves a spell in which love may be improbable but never impossible.